Roc

MW00936611

Sage Gardens Cozy Mystery Series

Cindy Bell

Copyright © 2015 Cindy Bell

All rights reserved.

ISBN-13: 978-1517787813

ISBN-10: 1517787815

Table of Contents

Chapter One

Samantha waved the cloud of smoke away from the top of the pan and cringed at the burnt creation in it.

"That's what I get for watching television while making breakfast." She shook her head and grabbed a potholder. Once she had a grip on the pan she eased it into the sink and added some water to cool it off. The sizzle was loud enough that she didn't hear the knock the first time. She turned off the water and heard the second set of knocks. Briefly she considered whether there was enough smoke for a neighbor to have called the fire department. That wouldn't be so bad, a few strapping young men in uniform. When she opened the door she found Jo. She tried not to look too disappointed as she looked at her slender friend dressed from head to toe in black.

"Wow! What did you burn?" Jo cringed as she was hit with the smell of the burnt breakfast.

"Bacon." Samantha sighed. "I can't say I'm a culinary whiz."

"Hm. Why don't you come to breakfast with me? There's something I want to talk to you about."

"Okay. Let me grab my purse." Samantha ducked back into the kitchen long enough to get her purse and make sure that the stove was turned off. Jo waited for her outside. Samantha walked through the living room and opened the windows. As she stepped out of the villa she smiled at Jo.

"Hopefully it'll be aired out by the time I get back."

"Burnt bacon should be a crime." Jo winked at her. "But look at the bright side, now we get to try out the new café they opened."

"Good point." Samantha nodded. "It's nice that management allowed it to be opened."

"Yes, I have to say, I moved into Sage Gardens for the quiet location, but all of the activities and amenities they offer has been nice."

As they walked down to the main office where the new café was, Samantha nodded and smiled to a few of the other residents of Sage Gardens. Jo however did not. In fact, most of the people that passed by didn't even offer her a second look. Jo was not the making friends type. Once they were settled at the café and placed their orders, Jo slid a brochure across the table.

"There is this amazing flower show that I am going to attend. I bought two tickets already, hoping that you would go with me."

"Really?" Samantha smiled. "That's so nice of you, Jo."

"Well, I might have had an ulterior motive." Jo grinned. "I am going there by train and I got a discount on the train tickets and flower show tickets because I bought tickets for two people together. See the package?" She pointed it out to Samantha. "But I would really like you to go with me. I know gardening isn't exactly your thing, but there are so many interesting plants to see at the show, I think you'll enjoy it."

"I'm sure I will." Samantha skimmed over the brochure. "I haven't been on a train in years. This will be so much fun."

"The food and drinks on the train can be really pricey and the train is quite old. But the scenery is gorgeous."

"You've been before?"

"Once, in my younger years. It'll be a bit of a walk down memory lane for me."

"How nice." Samantha met her friend's eyes. Despite the fact that they spent a good amount of time together, Samantha still didn't know Jo very well. Then again, she doubted that anyone knew Jo very well. Her nature was secretive.

"There's a fast train, but it's much more expensive and I thought overnight on the train would be fun to do again," Jo said.

"Sounds like it." Samantha smiled. "How long are we away for?"

"We leave in the afternoon, sleep on the train overnight and then go to the show and head back that night. So two nights," Jo explained. "Is that okay with you?"

"Sure, sounds like fun," Samantha said as she looked at the brochure. "Too bad we can't do this one." Samantha tapped another section of the brochure. "It comes with free food and drinks."

"Yes, that one requires four train tickets though." She lifted one shoulder in a half-shrug. "I only had one person to invite."

"Thanks for inviting me." Samantha smiled as her bacon and eggs arrived.

"Well, thanks for saying yes," Jo said happily and took a bite of her breakfast.

"I'm already looking forward to it. I haven't gotten to travel in a long time. I used to travel all the time."

"I know what you mean. I don't think I've left the state all year. That's so strange for me. It used to be an occupational perk." Jo smiled sheepishly. "It was once my goal to visit as many foreign countries as possible. Now, it's my goal just to go on a train ride."

"It's your goal right now. But who knows. First a train ride, then a plane ride, then maybe we'll even reach the moon."

"The moon?" Jo laughed.

"Well, you never know. You can go into space now. Could you imagine?"

"No thanks, I've got enough to deal with on earth." Jo shook her head.

"Good point." Samantha raised her cup of coffee. "Maybe we'll just stick to trains."

"I'll send you all of the details." Jo smiled.

"Great. I can't wait."

"I'm really looking forward to it, too." Jo finished her coffee.

"Before we go, though, you'll have to give me a crash course in flowers so that I don't call a daisy a daffodil."

"Come over a bit later to my garden and we'll go through it together." Jo stood up. "Thanks

Samantha." She met her friend's eyes. Samantha returned the gaze with a gentle smile. Jo was still getting used to the idea of having a friend, and though Samantha had friends over the years, she had never really had a best friend. Most women she knew couldn't understand her desire to be in dangerous situations for the sake of journalism. She didn't have to worry about that with Jo, who had the unusual history of being a cat burglar. Maybe they had danger in common, but Samantha didn't share her love of gardening. She made sure she was coated in bug spray before she headed over to Jo's garden.

***

After getting a basic overview of gardening from Jo, Samantha returned to her villa. As she walked towards the door she heard footsteps behind her. Out of habit she spun around, ready to defend herself.

"Easy there, tiger. I'm friendly." Eddy laughed. He adjusted his hat and met her eyes. "A little jumpy are you?"

"Well, you shouldn't be sneaking up on people." Samantha grinned. "You never know how I might react."

"I was hoping with an offer of lunch." Eddy angled his head to the side. "If you let me live that is."

"All right, I guess you can keep breathing." Samantha laughed. "So, you came over for lunch, hmm?"

"To offer to take you out to lunch." Eddy cleared his throat.

"That might be safer considering what I did to my kitchen this morning."

"Is everything okay?"

"It will be once it airs out."

"All right." He smiled. "I'll leave it at that."

"I'm going to be away for a few days."

"You are? Where are you going?" Eddy picked up her paper and handed it to her.

"I'm going on a train ride to a flower show.

Thank you." She took the paper from him and tossed it down on the table inside the door. Normally, she couldn't wait to tear into the paper and read the latest columns, but at the moment there was more on her mind than just whether the current crime journalist made a good effort.

"You are going to a flower show?" Eddy raised an eyebrow. "Didn't you kill a cactus once?"

"Never mind that. Jo invited me, and I can't wait to go."

"Well, that should be nice for you both." Eddy shook his head. "I can't say it would be my idea of a fun time."

"Oh!" Samantha's eyes widened. "What a good idea!"

"Huh?" Eddy glanced over his shoulder to see if someone stood behind him. "What idea?"

"You and Walt can go with us! There's a special package if you buy four tickets. If you and Walt come along, we can all enjoy free drinks and food on the train. This is perfect! Wait until Jo finds out. Oh no, wait, we'll surprise her. How long do you need to pack?"

"Wait just a minute." Eddy held up his hands and took a step back. "Who said I was going? And you haven't even asked Walt."

"Oh, sure you will go. Don't you want the chance to get to know Jo better?" Samantha offered her most charming smile, complete with wide eyes and a plucky wink. "We're going to have so much fun."

"Samantha, you're getting ahead of yourself. I don't know if this is such a good idea. Jo is a private person." Eddy frowned. "I don't want to invade her trip. Plus, I doubt Walt would go for it."

"He would if you do." Samantha crossed her arms. "You know that."

"Maybe, but again, Jo invited you, not me or Walt. Do you really think it's a good idea?"

"I think Jo needs to know that she has more than one friend." Samantha frowned. "You are her friend, aren't you?"

"That's not fair, Samantha. Jo and I may have our differences, but you know that she is my friend. She and Walt have been spending a lot of time together, too."

"So, it's a good idea." Samantha smiled.

"Just because Jo and I are friends that doesn't mean she wants us to tag along."

"Relax Eddy. I think I know women better than you. Do you want to go on the trip or not?"

He looked thoughtful. "Maybe."

"That's not an answer."

"What about lunch?" Eddy stepped into the villa and sniffed the air. "Oh wow, you did do a number in here didn't you?"

"Okay, Eddy I'll make you a deal. I will take you out to lunch, my treat, if you talk to Walt about going on the trip."

"Your treat?" Eddy stroked his fingers along his chin. "I could go for that."

"Only if you promise to talk to Walt." Samantha playfully poked her finger towards him.

"I promise, let's eat." Eddy sighed in defeat. "Why don't we go to the café in the courtyard?"

"I was just there for breakfast." Samantha laughed. "Why don't we just hit the sandwich shop on the corner?"

"Sounds good, they have fantastic soup." He held the door for Samantha as they stepped outside. "Samantha, there's something I've been meaning to ask you."

"Yes?" She glanced over at him as they walked to Eddy's car.

"When you worked as a crime journalist did you ever come across a man by the name of Peter Wilks?"

"Peter Wilks?" Samantha shook her head. "The name doesn't bring anyone to mind. But I've dealt with hundreds of people over the years, Eddy. Is there a reason you ask?"

"He's a friend of mine, just moved into town a

few blocks away. I mentioned you during a conversation and he swears that he worked on a story with you."

Samantha frowned as they got into the car. "I'm not sure. It's possible I guess," she replied once they were seated.

"He said that you were the most determined woman he ever met." Eddy cleared his throat. "So, there's no doubt in my mind that he was talking about you."

"Ha!" She grinned at him. "Well, we'll have to get together sometime. I remember stories better than I remember people, to be honest."

"It was something to do with funds disappearing from a charity that supported the families of fallen police officers."

"Is Peter a police officer?" Samantha asked. "Wait a minute, I think I do remember him. Oh." She smiled. "Yes, I'd love to get together with him."

Eddy raised an eyebrow as he started the car.

"I could invite him to lunch."

"Yes, please do," Samantha said with a dreamy smile on her lips.

***

"Peter said he'd be here in a few minutes," Eddy explained after hanging up the phone. "Let's order, I'm starving." Eddy gestured to the waitress.

"That's a little impolite, don't you think?" Samantha looked out through the front window of the shop. "We should wait for him."

"It seems to me that you're a little excited to see this guy. What's the story?" Eddy waved the waitress away.

"No story. He just gave me good information."

"Hm." Eddy nodded. "Well, if I don't find out from you I'm sure that I will find out from him."

"There's nothing to find out, Eddy." Samantha rolled her eyes.

"Here he is." Eddy stood up to greet his friend. Samantha smiled as Peter walked up to the table.

His short, brown hair was combed back from his forehead. He wore the same style she remembered him wearing, jeans and a button down top.

"Samantha." He smiled at her as he paused beside the table. "I can't believe it's really you, after all these years."

"It's me." Samantha giggled. Then she tried not to blush. "It's good to see you, Pete."

"You're still the only one who ever called me that." He shook his head and sat down beside her.

"Pete is a good name." Samantha leaned closer to him. "It's so nice to see you again. I'm sorry that we lost touch."

"Lost touch?" His expression hardened. "Is that what you call not returning my calls or e-mails, losing touch?"

Eddy sat down on the other side of Peter. Samantha's eyes widened.

"I'm sorry, I must have just gotten busy with a story."

"Must have." Peter winked, then he looked over at Eddy. "Are the cheese steaks good here?"

"Not bad, not the best." Eddy shrugged.

Samantha sat back against her chair. Her mind churned as she tried to remember whether she had a falling out with Peter. She recalled they had shared many coffees and a few meals. But she couldn't remember any arguments. She knew that the investigation became very intense at the end. Once they ordered their food Samantha decided to find out a little more about how things ended with Peter.

"What have you been up to since we worked on that case? Did you ever experience any consequences from the investigation?" she asked.

"Not really. I quit and went to work as a private investigator. I figured I'd rather work for myself than work for crooks."

"Now, not all cops are like that." Eddy narrowed his eyes. "You know that."

"Sure I do. You're the one exception, Eddy."

"That's right." Eddy laughed and nodded to the waitress as she brought their food.

"Well, you were one of the most honest police officers I ever worked with, Peter. If it wasn't for your information we never would have blown that story wide open."

"Yeah. We worked well together." Peter took a bite of his sandwich. Samantha's phone rang. She glanced down at it to see who it was.

"Oh, it's Jo, probably calling about the trip."

"You should ask her about Walt and me." Eddy wiped some crumbs from his hands.

"No, I want that to be a surprise." Samantha laughed. "I'll call her back in a bit."

"Are you going on a trip?" Peter finished his sandwich.

"Just for a couple of days, to a flower show."

"Are you kidding?" Peter asked.

"No." Samantha narrowed her eyes. "Do you know about my reputation as a plant murderer, too?"

"No. It's just that I'm going to the same show. I'm taking the train."

"So are we." Samantha's lips parted with shock. "What an amazing coincidence."

"Well, then maybe we'll see each other along the way. It was good to see you again, Samantha. Eddy, we'll have to get together soon." He nodded to Eddy, then stood up.

"Glad we had the chance to reconnect, Pete." Samantha stood up as well. Peter stared at her for a moment. His lips eased into a smile.

"Me too, Sam, me too. Maybe, we can keep in touch this time."

"I'd like that." Samantha nodded.

Eddy walked over to her as Peter left the shop. "You did a number on that guy, huh?"

"What?" Samantha looked over at him. "Did he say that?"

"He didn't have to." Eddy chuckled. "The heartbreak is written all over his face."

"That's not possible, we didn't even date."

Samantha shook her head.

"That doesn't mean he didn't fall in love, Sam."

"Eddy, you're being ridiculous."

"Am I?" He smiled. "I could easily see you so wrapped up in a story that you didn't notice the young cop mooning over you."

"Oh trust me, no one has ever mooned over me." Samantha laughed.

Chapter Two

Walt reached into his pocket and pulled out his cell phone. He checked the time. Eddy had called earlier to ask if he could stop by after lunch. Walt calculated the time it would take Eddy to get to his villa and waited on the porch for him. As another minute ticked by he squinted down the street. He saw the neighbor's Pekinese peeing on a bright red fire hydrant. A few ambitious people jogged down the sidewalk despite the heat. He didn't see Eddy. He looked back down at his phone to check the time. The shrill ring of the phone startled him so much that he almost dropped it.

"Eddy?"

"Yes, I'm on my way. Sorry, Walt, I got held up."

"All right, I'll be here. On the porch."

"Okay." Eddy hung up. Walt slid the phone back into his pocket. He sighed. He didn't like it when things didn't go as planned. A few minutes later Eddy walked up.

"What took so long?" Walt leaned against the railing.

"Sorry, I went out for lunch with Samantha. It took a little longer than I expected."

"Oh? How is she?"

"She's good. I had an old friend along with me for lunch, and apparently he and Samantha have quite a history." Eddy winked.

"Oh?" Walt stood up straight. "What kind of history?"

"She says they just worked together, but from his attitude I'd say that he expected more." Eddy shook his head. "Poor sap looked like he'd just been socked in the gut. The worst part is, she barely even remembers him. She claims there was never anything between them."

"Samantha doesn't seem like the type to be insensitive to anyone's feelings." Walt scratched the curve of his cheek. "Are you sure you're reading him right?"

"Trust me, when Samantha works a story, she works that story, and does nothing else. I don't think there's ever been a time that I've seen her notice someone's feelings while she was focused on an investigation."

"Huh." Walt tilted his head to the side. "You wouldn't be jealous would you, Eddy?"

"What?" Eddy took a step back. "You're crazy. I haven't been jealous of anyone or anything since I was twenty years old."

"Oh sure, okay." Walt nodded. "Take it easy, pal, it was just a question."

"A crazy question. Besides, Samantha and I are just friends."

"You're right, maybe I read too much into it." Walt smiled.

"Oh, you think you're real clever don't you?" Eddy laughed. "I see what you did there."

Walt shrugged. "Either way it's none of our business."

"The reason I came round is because Sam wants us to go on a train ride to a flower show with Jo."

"Huh. Wait, Jo invited us to go on a train?" Walt raised an eyebrow.

"Not exactly. She invited Samantha, and then Samantha invited us." Eddy shrugged. "If we go we get free food and drinks."

"Oh. Well I suppose that would be nice. Are you sure that Jo will be okay with us going though? She's never invited me anywhere before."

"There's a first for everything." Eddy shrugged. "Besides, it's time that Jo knew we were her friends, too. If that means inviting ourselves along on a trip, then that's what we will do."

"You're just in it for the free food, aren't you?" Walt smirked at him.

"I can tell you that I'm not opposed to free anything." Eddy laughed.

"What do you need on a train ride?" Walt frowned. "Lots of wipes, and hand sanitizer.

That's for sure."

"Yes, that would be good."

***

After Eddy left to talk with Walt, Samantha settled onto her couch and called Jo back.

"Sorry, I couldn't take your call, I was in the middle of lunch with Eddy and one of his friends."

"Oh, it's okay, I just wanted to make sure that you knew to pack a sunhat. It's going to be pretty hot."

"Thanks for the warning." She paused a moment. "Jo, something strange happened at lunch."

"What was it? Did Eddy order a salad?"

"Ha, no. Actually his old friend, was someone I once knew. I worked a story with him."

"It must have been nice to be reunited then."

"It would have been, but he seemed annoyed with me, like I'd done something wrong to him."

"Well, did you?"

"That's the thing, I don't think that I did. I don't remember doing anything wrong. Apparently, he called and e-mailed me and I didn't get back to him. I probably moved on to another story, and just didn't get back to him."

"It sounds like you made more of an impression on him than you realized." Jo sighed. "It happens sometimes. It's not your fault that he didn't get the hint."

"Want to know the worst part?" Samantha pressed the phone to her ear.

"What?"

"I can remember having a huge crush on him. It was actually pretty distracting to me while I worked on the story. I didn't usually go for police officers, but he was so idealistic, so determined to follow the letter of the law, but also to help people."

"So, he did make an impression." Jo cleared her throat.

"He did, it's just that I didn't remember any of

it until I saw him. That time of my life was so chaotic, it felt like everyone was out to get me. I guess the memory of Pete just got lost in the shuffle."

"Well, here's your chance." Jo's voice heightened with excitement. "It's a perfect time to reconnect. You're not actively working now, plenty of time to get to know each other again."

"It would be perfect, if he didn't seem to have a problem with me."

"Ouch."

"That's not even the worst part."

"There's more?" Jo asked eagerly.

"He's going on the same train to the same flower show!"

"Oh no! But wait, that could be great. It might give you two the chance to get to know each other again."

"Maybe." Samantha sighed. "So, that's my big adventure at lunch today."

"Sounds like quite an adventure. I'm looking

forward to the trip, even if your heartbroken ex is on it with us."

"He's not my ex, and I'm sure he's not heartbroken!"

"We'll see." Jo laughed.

Chapter Three

On the day of the trip, Samantha took a little extra time getting ready. Her mind kept drifting back to the fact that Peter would be on the train as well. Maybe she would have the chance to find out what happened. Once she was sufficiently primped Samantha grabbed her bag and walked towards the front door. When she opened it, she found Eddy and Walt poised to knock.

"Yes, right on time. I knew you would be, Walt, wasn't so sure about Eddy."

"I'll have you know I set two alarms," Eddy said. "Ready to go?"

"Yes. The cab is going to meet us at Jo's."

"Did you tell her about us going yet?" Eddy asked.

"No. I want it to be a surprise."

Walt cringed. "Not so sure it will be a good surprise."

"Relax, it'll be fine." Samantha locked her door. The three walked a few streets down to Jo's house. Samantha paused at the end of the driveway.

"Now remember, good attitudes and no complaining about flower talk."

"Why do I feel like I'm being coached?" Eddy shook his head. "We'll be fine don't worry, Samantha."

"Okay, let's get going." Samantha walked up the driveway to the door of Jo's villa. She reached up and knocked on the door. Walt and Eddy exchanged a glance.

"I think that we should have let her know first." Walt frowned. "I don't like surprises, I bet she doesn't either."

"Shh, it will be great!" Samantha waved at him to be silent. A moment later the door swung open and Jo stepped out. She had her overnight bag slung over her shoulder.

"Samantha, ready to go?" She smiled. Then

she noticed the two men who stood behind Samantha. Her smile reduced considerably. "Walt and Eddy, what are you doing here?"

"See!" Walt frowned and adjusted the strap of his small bag.

"We're going along for the ride." Eddy sighed. "We don't have to come if you don't want us to. Samantha thought it would be a good idea."

"Oh did she?" Jo narrowed her eyes.

"So we can get the discounted package, the free food and drinks!" Samantha's tone was very enthusiastic.

"I guess that will be a good thing. We'll have two rooms?" She looked at Eddy and Walt.

"Yes, of course." Eddy nodded.

"I hope it's not a bother to you, Jo, to have us go along," Walt said.

"No, it's not." Jo looked at Samantha. "Samantha, may I speak to you for a moment?"

"Sure you can." Samantha dropped her bag by Walt and Eddy's. "Give us a minute." She followed

Jo into her villa. Jo closed the door and fixed Samantha with a frown.

"Why would you do this to me?"

"What do you mean?"

"I mean, you could have at least asked me about it instead of springing this on me."

"If I had, would you have said no?" Samantha asked. "I honestly didn't think it would bother you."

"I probably wouldn't have said no, but that's not the point. The point is I would have at least known what to expect. I like to be able to prepare for things."

"That's funny."

"Why is it funny?" Jo threw her hands in the air with exasperation.

"I'm sorry, it's just that Walt told me that you wouldn't like to be surprised and he was right. He likes to prepare for things, too."

"I think most people do." Jo put her hands on her hips. "I thought it would be just you and me on the trip."

Samantha's eyes widened. "Oh Jo, I didn't realize that you were looking forward to it just being us. I mean it's usually just us. I thought you might want to see that Eddy and Walt are your friends, too."

"I know that Eddy and Walt are my friends, too." Jo shrugged. "Just not quite the same as you are."

"Well, maybe after this trip they will be." Samantha smiled. "It's worth a shot isn't it?"

"I suppose it is." Jo sighed. "Only for you, Samantha."

"It was a good idea, admit it."

"We'll see after the trip." She picked up her bag. "Looks like the cab is here," Samantha said as she opened the door and saw the cab pulled up at the end of the driveway. Walt had his and Samantha's bags in his hands. Eddy reached out to take Jo's.

"Let me get that."

"Oh, that's okay, I can carry it."

"I know you can, but I insist." Eddy took the strap of the bag.

"All right." Jo smiled.

"See." Samantha nudged her with her elbow. "Not so bad having them around, hmm?"

"Maybe not." Jo laughed.

***

Jo gave the instructions to the driver while Eddy and Walt stowed their bags. Walt did a quick wipe down of the inside of the cab before he allowed anyone to get inside.

"It's a bit tight in here, isn't it?" Walt shifted over further on the bench seat of the cab.

"Just try not to breathe." Eddy smiled at Walt. Samantha and Jo wedged in on the other side.

"Might want to get used to it, I'm pretty sure the rooms on the train won't be much bigger." Samantha patted Eddy's knee. "We're going to be in close contact for the next nineteen hours."

"Actually, it's only eighteen." Walt nodded. "I checked."

"Trust me it'll feel like longer." Eddy grimaced. "I was stuck on a train once for three days. It felt like a year."

"Why were you stuck on it?" Jo looked past Samantha to meet his eyes.

"It's a long story, but basically I was following a suspect. I fell asleep, and woke up about five states away from where I was supposed to be. Then I had to take the train all the way back only to find out that my suspect was never on the train in the first place." He shook his head. "It was not my greatest hour."

"That's what you get for sleeping on the job." Samantha grinned.

"You've always got something funny to say, Samantha, but I bet you've had your fair share of embarrassing moments while on a stakeout," Eddy mused.

"Maybe Peter knows some of them," Jo

chimed in.

Samantha looked from Eddy to Jo. "If he does, you're not going to find out." She joked.

For the rest of the trip to the train station Samantha's antics as a crime reporter was the main topic of conversation. When they pulled up to the train station Samantha turned to Eddy and smiled. "Pay the cab, Eddy," she said as she gave him a light smack on the knee.

"Me?" He sputtered and reached for his wallet. "How much?" He peered at the driver. As Eddy settled the fare, Jo and Samantha climbed out of the cab. Walt stepped out of the other side. He immediately began wiping down his trousers and anything else that might have touched the interior of the cab with a disposable disinfectant wipe.

"All clean?" Eddy slid out behind him.

"Can I ever be clean again after that ride?" Walt cringed and tossed the wipe in a nearby trashcan. The train station was small, but crowded.

"Jo and I already have our tickets, so we'll wait for you two on the platform."

"Here, just make sure you give them this code so that we can get the group discount." Jo handed Eddy a slip of paper.

"Will do." Eddy nodded and walked towards the ticket window. Walt followed after him. He clutched his bag so tight that his fingers were white from the pressure. Samantha linked her arm through Jo's and walked towards the platform. It was crowded with people saying goodbye and people waiting for the train. Samantha leaned close to Jo.

"Looks like I might not even get to see Pete on this trip."

"He might be hard to spot." Jo nodded. "I didn't expect it to be this busy."

"Must be the warm weather. Everyone has somewhere they want to go."

"You might be right." Jo looked towards Eddy and Walt as they joined the line. "I still wish that you had told me about Eddy and Walt joining us."

"Why? Would you have packed something cute?" Samantha winked at her.

"No, of course not. It's just I've been looking forward to this trip, and you know how Eddy can get. To him I will always be a criminal."

"Eddy's stubborn, but he's been coming around lately, don't you think? Besides, one of the main reasons he agreed was because I pointed out that he would have the chance to get to know you better."

"Really?" she asked doubtfully. "I don't know why."

"Maybe they enjoy their time with you. What's so wrong with that?" Samantha pulled away from her and stepped to the edge of the platform. "But you're right, I should have told you the truth and asked if it was okay. I guess the real reason I didn't was because I thought you would refuse the idea. I just wanted the four of us to have some fun together. It seems like the only time we spend any amount of time together is when something goes wrong. Have you noticed that?"

Jo laughed. "Yes, I guess I have noticed that."

"It'll be fun, I promise," Samantha assured her.

"It doesn't look like too much fun for them right now." Jo tipped her head towards the long line.

***

The line was about ten people deep when Eddy and Walt stepped into it. More people filed in right behind them. As they waited Eddy looked around at the crowd. It was instinct for him to always assess his environment. There was quite a mixture of people from business people to young teens. Everyone appeared fairly under control, but there were a few who were not so steady on their feet. The train station had a small restaurant attached. Eddy guessed that some of the passengers had enjoyed a few drinks over lunch.

"Oh, that is disgusting," Walt's voice rattled with horror. Eddy's attention snapped right back to him. He looked around for what Walt saw.

"What is it?"

"Just look," Walt barely whispered.

Eddy followed Walt's line of sight. He noticed a man in a pair of jeans and a t-shirt. Eddy didn't see anything that disgusted him.

"His hands," Walt hissed.

Eddy looked down at the man's hands. He saw that there were several scabs on his skin which he picked at until they flaked off and fell onto the ground.

"Oh." Eddy tried not to roll his eyes.

"Why would anyone do that, in public no less?" Walt shook his head.

"Just try not to look. We're almost at the front."

Walt sighed. He didn't look away from the man, or his hands. Eddy glanced over at the edge of the platform. He saw that Samantha hovered near the edge of the platform. He was about to open his mouth to admonish her, but before he could she moved away from the edge.

"Next?"

Eddy turned towards the ticket agent. Her eyes drooped and her lips were tight.

"Busy day?" Eddy said.

"Very. The train is going to be very crowded."

"We'd like to purchase two tickets under this code, I believe that should make it the Buy Four and Save More deal." He slid the piece of paper with the code on it towards her.

"Oh yes, this is a good deal." She hit a few buttons on her keyboard then gave Eddy the total. Eddy reached into his wallet.

"You're not using a credit card, are you?" Walt grimaced. "Credit cards are best used only in emergencies, Eddy, you should know that."

"Relax Walt, I handle my finances just fine, but I am going to use cash." He winked at the woman behind the counter as he handed her the money. "Retired accountant, you know how numbers guys are."

"Sure, sure." She laughed. "Here are your tickets. Just make sure that you keep your vouchers for the free food and drink with you, all right?"

"We will." Eddy smiled. "They're not going to leave my side." He took the tickets and vouchers from her. As they turned to walk back towards the platform, Eddy narrowed his eyes. "What's going on over there?" He raised an eyebrow. A small crowd had formed around the area of the platform where Samantha and Jo waited.

***

Samantha sighed and checked her watch. "It is taking them forever."

"That's why I bought ours ahead. There's some kind of boxing tournament not far from the flower show, so there's a lot of people taking the train."

"So, what flowers are you most excited to see at the show?" Samantha did her best to sound interested.

"I'd like to learn more about orchids. They are difficult to grow in this climate, very delicate."

"Are you going to try to grow some?" Samantha's question was interrupted by a loud bang. She jumped at the sound and spun around to see a woman who stood in the middle of the platform. Her large suitcase was flat on the ground. Samantha guessed that she had dropped it. She walked over to help her retrieve it. As she got closer to the woman she could see that her features were pale and speckled with sweat. Her eyes were tightened as if she tried to hold back tears. Several other people gathered to see if the woman was all right.

"Miss, are you okay?" Samantha picked up her suitcase. The woman took it from her and nodded.

"Yes, sorry if I startled you." When she spoke the smell of alcohol drifted right under Samantha's nose. She was one of the people that had enjoyed a few too many drinks at the restaurant.

"Are you sure you're okay?" Samantha frowned.

"I'm fine really, I'm sorry to bother you." She clung tightly to her suitcase.

"Are you with anyone?" Samantha glanced around. "A friend, your husband?"

"No one." The woman dabbed at her eyes. "I'm alone. But I'm fine. I just want to get on the train."

Samantha nodded. Jo steered her away by the elbow.

"She doesn't want any help, Samantha. Best to leave her alone." The crowd began to disperse.

"She seems pretty drunk." Samantha grimaced. "I hope she can make it onto the train."

"That's her choice." Jo clenched her jaw. "I have no patience for drunks. As Samantha and Jo walked away from the woman she saw that Eddy and Walt were ready with their tickets. They walked over to Samantha and Jo.

"What's going on?" Eddy tilted his head

towards the woman who still struggled with her suitcase.

"Oh, she seems a little drunk." Jo frowned. "I have a feeling this might not be as peaceful a ride as I had hoped."

"Don't worry," Eddy said. "Walt and I will keep things nice and boring for you."

Chapter Four

"Time to board." Jo pointed to the groups gathered near the entrance of the cars. The four walked over to join the line by theirs. As they waited to board Samantha looked around at the crowd.

"Looking for someone?" Eddy asked and quirked his brow.

"Yes." Samantha continued to search.

"Peter?"

"What?" Samantha looked at him. "No! That's not who I'm looking for. I'm looking for the woman from the platform. I just wanted to make sure she gets on the train okay."

"You're a bleeding heart." Eddy shook his head.

"Nothing wrong with looking out for your fellow human beings." Samantha sighed. "Right, Jo?"

"Actually, I agree with Eddy on this. Anyone who would get that drunk before they even get on the train deserves whatever they get." Jo frowned.

"Thank you, Jo." Eddy tipped his hat.

"It's nice to see you two agree on something." Walt smiled. "But you should both be a little more compassionate."

"What do you mean?" Eddy stepped aside to let Jo and Samantha board in front of him.

"Alcoholism is not easy to shake. Too many people think it's a choice, but the numbers show that it's a disease. Just something to think about. If the woman had a heart condition would you find her so repulsive?"

"I never said anything about repulsive." Eddy shook his head.

"Maybe you have a point, Walt, but I've never known anyone who has got a heart condition that caused an accident," Jo said.

"She's getting on a train, not in a car." Walt stepped up onto the train as well.

"Our room is down this corridor." Eddy nodded his head to the right.

"Ours is this way." Jo pointed in the opposite direction.

"Let's meet in the dining car in a couple of hours after we get settled." Samantha waved to Eddy as the crowd swept her and Jo down the corridor.

***

Eddy pushed open the door to the room he would share with Walt. The moment he did, he regretted it. The space was tiny, but that was not the problem. The problem was the smell in the room. It smelled like something had been left behind and ignored for a very long time. Walt poked his head in.

"Oh, no, no." He shook his head. "I can't stand for this."

"Walt, I doubt they're going to let us change rooms. It's so packed on this train."

"Don't worry, I don't want to change rooms. I

want to clean this one." Walt stepped right in and opened his bag. He pulled out a few wipes and cleaning supplies. Then he looked under the furniture. Eddy could only stand back and watch as Walt searched the entire room.

"Aha! Here it is!" Walt held up a bag that he had pulled out from under the bed. "Someone left behind some rotten apples."

"I think there's a joke there." Eddy grinned.

"Here you go." Walt held out the bag. "It's your job to take out the trash."

"Is that a cop crack?" Eddy asked as he took the bag. "I'll find a trashcan far away from here for this."

The corridor had cleared from the initial rush of people in search of their rooms. Eddy noticed a man at the end of the corridor. He appeared to be struggling with the door to his room. Eddy walked past him into the next car of the train to dispose of the rotten apples. As he brushed past the man he noticed that the hair on the back of his neck was soaked with sweat. The temperature on the train was very cool. He looked at the man a moment longer.

"What is that smell?" The man looked up, annoyed.

"Sorry, found it in my room." Eddy held up the bag.

"Well, get it out of here will you?" The man was finally able to open the door. He ducked inside his room and closed his door. Eddy shook his head and moved into the next car of the train. He threw the apples out in the trash and turned around to head back to his room. By the time he stepped back in, the room smelled like lemon and Walt was perched on the edge of his bed.

"Wow, you work fast."

"Better huh?" Walt smiled.

"Much." Eddy started to walk in.

"Uh, shoes off!" Walt pointed at his feet.

"Seriously?" Eddy sighed and slid his shoes off. "This is going to be a long eighteen hours."

"Really, it's only seventeen now."

***

Samantha looked around the room. "Well, it's cozy."

"You could call it that." Jo grinned. "We will make it work. Wait until you see the view." She opened the shade on the window. "There's this amazing overpass, the mountains are enough to make you want to become a painter."

"Sounds gorgeous." Samantha settled into the seat by the window. "I really think this was a great idea, Jo."

"So far, so good." Jo unzipped her bag and rifled through it. "I'm sorry that you haven't seen Pete yet. Maybe you'll see him in the dining car."

"I'm not sure if I even want to see him."

"Oh, you do, you know you do." She laughed.

"I have to admit that I'm curious." Samantha frowned. "But I doubt with the amount of people on this train that I will run into him. I guess I'll leave it up to fate."

"Good plan." Jo grabbed her by the hand. "My

plan is to get you in the dining car where he might be able to spot you!"

Samantha laughed as Jo pulled her down the corridor towards the dining car. Samantha caught herself checking the faces of all of the people she passed to see if it was Peter. She noticed the woman they had seen on the platform. She stood near the end of the corridor close to a room door. Samantha lowered her eyes as she wanted to avoid a potential conversation. When Samantha stole a peek in her direction, it seemed to her that the woman checked every person who walked by as well. Samantha wondered for a moment who she was looking for since she had stated that she was alone. Then she brushed the thought from her mind.

"Stay close." Jo slid open the door to the dining car. Samantha stayed right behind her. There were only a few open tables left. The bar which also served as the food counter was packed with people. Jo found the closest table and sat down. Samantha sat down beside her.

"Well, now that we're here we better not get up." Samantha laughed.

***

The dining car rocked back and forth as Eddy stepped into it. He grabbed the wall to steady himself.

"Oh here, you're going to need this." Walt held out a disinfectant wipe.

"Walt, give it a rest. We're going to be stuck on this train with all of these people for a long time. Just relax."

"If only I could." Walt frowned. Eddy shook his head and walked further into the dining car. The place was packed, as was the rest of the train. He didn't see a single empty booth.

"Over here!" Samantha waved her hand in the air from a booth near the counter.

"Oh good, they've saved us a spot." Eddy led with his right shoulder in an attempt to force his way through the crowd. "Excuse me, excuse me." He was about half way there when he realized that

Walt was no longer right behind him. He turned back to see Walt staring at the crowd with great trepidation. Rather than annoyance, Eddy's demeanor softened with sympathy. He often forgot how difficult it was for Walt to function outside of his safe home and routine. He moved back through the crowd.

"Come on. I'll get you to where you need to be." He grabbed the sleeve of Walt's suit jacket and guided him through the crowd. When they reached the table, Jo smiled at them.

"Do you feel like a sardine?"

"I think that sardines have more room." Eddy grinned. He sat down at the table. Walt took a moment to make sure that his seat was clean and then he sat down as well.

"It's worth it." Samantha tapped the table with her fingertips. "We are going to have a great time."

"Plenty of opportunity to people watch." Jo smiled.

"I'll be having fun when the free food and drinks start flowing." Eddy chuckled. "It's pretty crowded up at the bar. Why don't all of you give me your vouchers and I'll go up and get our drinks?"

"That's very kind of you, Eddy, thank you." Samantha handed him her voucher. Jo nodded and handed him hers as well.

"Walt?" Eddy raised an eyebrow.

"I'm not sure if I want to drink anything from here." Walt cringed. "Do you think they wash those glasses?"

"Of course they do, Walt." Samantha patted the back of his hand.

"No, I mean really wash them, not just rinse them out in the sink." Walt sighed. "Those glasses could be covered in germs."

"Don't worry, if they are the alcohol will kill them." Eddy clapped him on the back.

"Ouch." Walt frowned. "I asked you not to do that."

"Sorry. Habit. So, are you going to give me the voucher or not?"

"Sure, all right. Here it is." Walt handed it to him.

"Great, I'll be right back with drinks for all of us." Eddy turned towards the bar. When he saw the crowd there he amended his statement. "All right, maybe not right back. It could be a while."

As Eddy lined up with the rest of the customers, he was relieved that Walt did not join him. People were pressed so close together that Eddy could hear snippets of their conversation, and feel their breath on him. He was sure that Walt would not be able to deal with it. As the line moved forward Eddy found himself beside a man who held the attention of several people in line. With nothing better to do, Eddy listened in.

"I need a little liquid courage for this trip." The man chuckled. He appeared young to Eddy. Perhaps in his twenties. "I'm finally going to pop the question," he said as he held up a diamond ring. "I've even bought the rock."

"Oh yeah?" another man barked out. "Why would you want to go and do a stupid thing like that?"

"I know, I know, it's not manly to be in love. But this girl, this woman, is the most amazing woman I've ever known. We were forced into a long distance relationship, but now I can finally cross the distance and ask her the question that I've been dreaming of asking for so long. I cannot wait to hear, Ryan Barker will you take Leila Wall to be your lawfully wedded wife."

"Well, good luck, chap, I guess, if that's what you want." The other man shrugged and turned back to the bar. Eddy smiled to himself. He could remember the first time he thought he was in love, and the first woman that he thought hung the moon. It was a heady, wonderful time, until she didn't feel the same way. He hoped the young man would get to avoid that kind of heartbreak.

"Good luck." He nodded to the man.

"Thanks. I'll probably need it." He laughed as a barmaid finally walked over to take Eddy's order. Eddy balanced the drinks in his hands and walked back towards his table. It took a little maneuvering, but he managed to reach it without spilling a drop. He set the drinks down at the table and settled into his chair.

"That was a jungle. I have a feeling we're not going to be seeing as much of this free food and drink as we hoped."

"Well, it always tastes better when it's free." Jo took a long swig of her drink.

"I agree." Eddy held up his drink then swallowed down half of it. Walt rubbed the rim of his glass clean with a tissue and then took a sip. Samantha's drink sat untouched. Her gaze locked to a man who had just walked into the dining car. Peter Wilks weaved his way between people that waited in line at the bar. He didn't get in line. Instead, he walked all the way to the other side of the dining car. There were no open tables. He leaned against the wall. Samantha bit into her bottom lip. She wondered if she should invite him to sit at their table. Just as she was about to dismiss the idea, Eddy shot his hand up into the air.

"Peter! Hey Peter!" He waved his hand. Samantha instinctively sunk down in her chair. She knew there was no getting out of it now.

Peter raised his hand enough in the air to silence Eddy, but he made no move to walk over. Samantha lowered her eyes. All of the hopes she had of rekindling any kind of connection with Peter burst. He clearly didn't want anything to do with her, and was even avoiding Eddy because she was there. Whatever she had done to hurt him, must have been pretty bad.

"I don't think he wants to sit with us, Eddy," Samantha said.

"He probably just doesn't want to walk all the way back across the dining car."

Jo leaned across the table. "Is that him? Is that the famous Peter?"

"Yup, that's him all right. What has she been telling you?" Eddy asked.

"Nothing much, just that she broke his heart."

"Okay stop, that's enough." Samantha shook her head. Her cheeks burned bright red from her friends' comments and from the disappointment of Peter not being interested.

Eddy coughed, then took another swallow of his drink. "Don't worry about him. He's probably working a case."

"On the train?" Samantha raised an eyebrow.

"Can you think of another reason that he would be going to a flower show?" Eddy asked.

"You know, Eddy, there are plenty of men who enjoy horticulture as much as women." Jo finished her drink and set her glass down. "Just because you're not in touch with your nourishing side, doesn't mean other men aren't."

"In touch with my nourishing side?" Eddy joked. "I wouldn't think that I had one to get in touch with."

"Oh, you do." Jo smiled. "Everyone does."

Samantha couldn't keep her eyes off Peter. He

continued to simply lean up against the wall. How was that more important than catching up with old friends?

"It's so crowded in here." Walt shifted in his seat. "I don't think I can take it much longer. The air is getting so thick."

"Just try to relax, Walt. This is a good exercise for you, right?"

"Exercise?" Walt frowned. "This isn't going to make me any calmer about crowds, trust me. When you combine the speed of this train with the amount of people in this particular car, the result you get is disaster."

"Are you saying the train might crash?" Samantha raised an eyebrow.

"Walt, stop scaring her. Samantha, the train isn't going to crash." Jo shook her head.

"You're absolutely right, Jo. Samantha, the train is not likely to crash. Not many trains actually crash, as in collide with other things. However, they do derail much more frequently, which is actually worse than crashing. If a train crashes it's likely that only the front of the train is impacted, not many lives lost. If a train derails, then there is the potential for all of the cars to tip, twist, explode." Walt shrugged. "Many more lives lost. So, as Jo said, the train is not likely to crash."

"Walt!" Jo set her drink down hard on the table. "This is supposed to be a fun getaway. Not a lecture on how we might die."

"Walt has a point." Samantha looked over the crowd teeming with very intoxicated people. "I've been in enough dangerous situations to know when it's time to leave. If this many people are drinking this much alcohol there is a good chance a fight will break out."

"Well, is it going to be a fight or a crash?" Jo stood up and put her hands on her hips.

"Uh, remember it's more likely to be a derailment..."

"Walt!" Samantha and Jo spoke his name at the same time. Walt jumped in reaction to the attention.

"What?" He looked over at Eddy. "Did I say something wrong?"

"I have an idea. Why don't we all go back to the girls' room and play some cards?" Eddy produced a deck of cards from his pocket. "I brought a deck just in case we had the chance to play."

"Now, that sounds like a great idea." Jo's lips curled upward with confidence. "I can beat all of you in a hand of rummy."

As a group they made their way through the crowd and out of the dining car. The moment they were out of the dining car the noise died down. The corridors were actually fairly empty.

"I guess everyone is either in the dining car, or holed up in their rooms." Samantha sighed with relief. "Not much else to do on a train."

"So far this trip isn't exactly going as planned."

"Don't fret, Jo, we're going to have fun." Samantha hooked her arm through Jo's. "Once we're playing cards, you won't even remember the noise of the dining car. You'll get your peaceful trip."

"In here." Jo tilted her head towards the door of their room. "There's not a lot of room I'm afraid."

Eddy poked his head inside. "I'm sure we can all fit."

Samantha sat on the seat near the window and Jo sat on the single bed opposite Samantha so they could look at the view. Eddy sat on the end of Jo's bed and Walt sat next to Samantha. They used the small table between the bed and seat to deal the cards.

"I'll deal." Eddy began to shuffle the cards.

"Oh dear, you're doing that wrong. May I see the cards?" Walt tried to grab the cards from Eddy's hands.

"Walt relax, they're just cards," Eddy said.

"But if you don't shuffle them well, the entire game will be ruined."

"Eddy, just let him shuffle." Samantha offered him a sweet smile. "It's for the best."

"All right, all right, but I get the next deal."

"Good, then pay attention to how I shuffle, that way you can do it right next time."

Jo leaned close to Samantha.

"Are you doing okay?" She met Samantha's eyes.

"Yes, I'm all right."

"I'm sorry that Peter didn't want to talk."

"It's for the best." Samantha shrugged. "What would we even really have to talk about? It was silly of me to ever expect that whatever I did in the past could simply be swept under the rug. Besides, I'm having plenty of fun playing cards with my four friends." She flashed a smile in Walt's direction. He didn't notice as his mind was on Eddy's sloppy dealing.

"That's two cards not one." Walt pointed to Jo's pile of cards.

"Oops. So, I'll skip her on the next round."

"No!" Walt shook his head. "No, that makes it unfair because she's not getting as random cards as she should. That card should be Samantha's. If you just skip her next time you will be throwing off the entire balance of the game."

"Walt." Jo frowned. "It's okay."

"No, he's right." Eddy smiled at Walt. "Here, let's fix it this way." He picked up the top card in Jo's pile and moved it to Samantha's. "How's that?"

Walt sighed with relief. "Better. Thanks Eddy."

Eddy shrugged. "Hey, when I beat you I don't want you making any claims that I threw the game."

Walt grinned. "No chance that you're going to manage that."

"We'll see," Eddy said confidently.

"Boys, do remember this is just a game." Samantha picked up her cards.

"To you it's a game, to us, it's a battle." Walt

picked up his cards as well. As the four took their turns the train rumbled on. The noise of the dining car was blocked out by the door of the room and the roar of the train.

Samantha glanced up as the train shifted a little around a curve. "Oh look, Jo!" She pointed out the window at the mountains that rose beyond it.

"We're coming up to the overpass." Jo smiled. "It's worth the train ride, just for that view."

Samantha stared out the window, until Walt's voice drew her attention.

"Your turn, Samantha."

Samantha played her turn, and returned her attention to the window.

"Oh yeah, this is it. Read them and weep!" Eddy prepared to lay his cards down on the table. Just as he did, the train lurched hard. The brakes ground and shrieked. Eddy's cards fluttered across the table. Walt jumped up from the seat.

"It's a derailment!" Walt exclaimed.

The train lurched again. Walt lost his balance and tumbled back into Samantha.

"Hang on!" Eddy grabbed onto a hook on the wall.

Jo stood up from the bed. "It's not a derailment, the train is safe. It's just stopped, suddenly." She peered out the window. "I don't know why."

Walt managed to get back to his feet. "I'm sorry, Samantha, are you all right?"

"That's okay. Walt. I'm okay." Samantha stood up as well and joined Jo at the window.

"Let's see what's going on." Eddy walked to the door. He opened it and was greeted by quite a commotion. Several train attendants ran down the corridor followed by a security officer.

"Something major is going on." Eddy glanced back into the room. "I think that we better stay inside until they figure out what is happening."

"Why would the train stop here?" Jo looked out the window. "We're not even close to a station.

We're right on the edge of the mountains."

"There's only a few possible reasons. Maybe some engine trouble," Walt suggested.

"Engine trouble wouldn't make them put on the brakes like that." Eddy shook his head.

"Well, the important thing is that we're all safe." Walt sighed.

"That's true, but I want to know what's happening. What if it's a train robbery?" Samantha's eyes widened.

"Like in the old west movies?" Jo laughed.

"I'm serious. Why couldn't it happen today?"

"Sam, I think you're letting your imagination get the better of you." Eddy peeked out the door again into the corridor. "It's clear out here now."

"Well, we can't just sit here. Let's go see what's happening," Samantha encouraged.

"Ugh, do you know how many investigations I've been on that got gummed up because some curious neighbor got in the middle of it?" Eddy said. "We should stay put and let security and the staff handle it."

"Samantha could be right though. If there is something criminal happening on the train I don't want to just sit here and wait for it to get to us." Jo shook her head. "We know how to stay out of the way. Let's go take a look."

Eddy looked at Walt. "What do you think?"

"I think I have to know what's happening. Let's go." Walt slid past the others and right out into the corridor. Samantha followed behind him, with Jo behind her. Eddy took a look up and down the corridor then fell into step behind them.

Chapter Five

The corridor remained empty as the four friends walked down it. If there were any other passengers disturbed by the sudden stop of the train they were not brave enough to emerge from their rooms. Samantha's heart fluttered as she heard the intercom system crackle to life.

"Passengers, we apologize for the delay. We will be back on schedule shortly. Please remain in your rooms for the moment."

"Oh dear, maybe we should go back?" Walt looked up at the speaker.

"No look." Samantha gestured to a train staff member that entered the corridor. "Let's see what we can find out." She broke away from the group and hurried to meet the man in the middle of the corridor.

"Excuse me, do you know what happened?" Samantha asked.

"Ma'am, just go back to your room. Nothing

to see here. We will be on our way again soon."

"Please, I just want to know that everyone is safe." Samantha bit into her lip nervously. "Should we leave the train?"

"No one leaves until we move the body." His tone became stern. "There is nowhere for anyone to go. We are right alongside the mountains."

"Body?" Samantha took a slight step back. "What do you mean body? Is someone dead?"

"Oh, now you've made me say more than I should have. Do you want me to get fired?" His cheeks reddened. "Please excuse me."

"I'm not going to cause you any trouble. I just want to know what's going on, that's all. Was someone on the tracks?" Samantha shifted her body in front of his when he tried to step around her.

He sighed and shook his head. "Look, sometimes people come on a train, not to get to their destination, if you know what I mean."

"Are you saying someone jumped off the

train?" Samantha's chest tightened. "Who? Was it a passenger? A staff member?"

"I can't tell you that. What I can tell you is that the train will be moving again soon. We just need everyone to be as patient as possible so that the local police can complete their investigation. Okay? So, please go back to your room, and do your best to remain calm."

Eddy, Walt and Jo caught up with her. The four of them blocked off the corridor.

"Anything I can do to help?" Eddy offered his hand. "I'm a retired police officer."

The staff member ignored his hand. "What I need all of you to do is return to your rooms. If you continue to cause trouble you will be forced off the train at the next station." He brushed past them and stomped down the corridor.

"Yikes, he's touchy." Samantha stared after him. "He gave me the impression that someone committed suicide by jumping off the train."

"How awful." Jo ran her hand across her

stomach.

Eddy peered out through the nearby window. "Looks like they've called in some local police."

"We'd better get back to the rooms before security catches us in the corridor." Walt pointed to a group of men that were about to enter the corridor.

"You're right." Eddy nodded. "Let's all stick to one room for now though."

As they walked back towards the room, Samantha noticed another person who was in the corridor. She stood near a room door, but she didn't try to open it. Samantha recognized her right away as the woman that she had first encountered on the platform. She was as white as a sheet.

"Did you find out who it was?" Her breath was still laced with alcohol, so much that Samantha had to cover her nose to block out the smell.

"I'm sorry?" Samantha said.

"The man who died, do you know his name?"

"We didn't even know that it was a man. The staff are being very tight-lipped." Samantha frowned.

Eddy studied the woman. "You should go back into your room."

"Oh no, this isn't mine. Not my room," she muttered.

"Do you need some help finding your room?" Walt offered his arm. Samantha was shocked by the gesture, but kept silent about it.

"No, I'm fine. I just wondered if you knew his name." She sighed.

"Let's keep moving." Jo tilted her head back over her shoulder. The group of men continued down the corridor in their direction. "I don't want to get thrown off the train."

"All right." Walt frowned. His eyes remained on the woman a moment longer, then he nodded. They continued down the corridor to the room. Once inside, Eddy sunk down on the end of the bed.

"I guess we have ourselves a real situation here."

"If it's a suicide, then as sad as it is the train should be on its way soon enough," Samantha said.

"If." Eddy lofted an eyebrow.

"Eddy, don't go looking for a case where there isn't one." Samantha crossed her arms. "Until we know something for sure we have to assume it was suicide."

Eddy glanced out the window. "Now, what is he doing out there?"

"Who?" Samantha tried to see past him out the window.

"You three stay put. I'll be back. I'm going to find out what's going on."

"Eddy wait." Jo started to move towards him.

"Don't worry, I won't get us thrown off the train." Eddy was out the door before any of them could stop him.

***

Eddy saw a few people in the corridor. They were getting restless. There hadn't been another announcement to satisfy the curiosity of the passengers. He blended in with the group and moved slowly towards the next train car. He was determined to find out what had happened. He noticed a staff member exit through a door at the end of the train. He quickly went to that door. He found that the door was unlatched. Eddy pushed it open and paused to see if it would set off an alarm. Nothing happened, so he stepped down through the door.

The police and train security were a few feet away on the rocks. Eddy did his best to stay out of their line of sight as he moved towards the man he spotted through the window. Once he reached the point of exposure, he did his best to appear as if he belonged there. He thrust his shoulders back and walked with purpose. It was his cop walk. Eddy walked towards the tangle of local police. He paused just outside of the group. He wasn't about to interrupt them and alert them to his presence.

Peter walked up beside him.

"Don't even try to talk to them, trust me."

Eddy looked over at Peter. "Why not?"

"They're not friendly. I already tried to get some information and they threatened to have me locked up."

"Did you get anything?" Eddy pushed his hat up along his forehead and looked directly into Peter's eyes.

"I overheard the name of the victim."

"Victim? Was it a murder?"

"If it was they're not treating it like one. They say that he jumped off from the rear outdoor viewing platform. But I don't think they have a clue what they're doing. They were all just in a rush to get the body away from the tracks so they can get the train rolling again."

"What's the name of the victim?"

"Ryan Barker."

"Ryan Barker," Eddy repeated the name as he

recognized it immediately. He thought about mentioning that he had seen the victim on the train, but decided against it.

Peter sighed and shook his head as a sheet was draped over the body. "They're not collecting any forensic evidence. Nothing. They're just rushing right through this. I guess it's for the best." He shrugged.

"How could that be for the best?" Eddy narrowed his eyes. "Do they have any proof that it was a suicide?"

"There's been some mumblings about a note being left in Ryan's room. I haven't been able to confirm that though. Like I said, they're not friendly." He tilted his head towards a police officer that walked towards them. "Get ready for an argument."

"What are you two doing out here? Are you passengers?" The officer glared at them.

"No, we're mountain goats." Peter scowled at him. Eddy glanced over at Peter with some shock.

"Watch your mouth. You're interfering with an investigation."

"Officer, I just wanted to offer my services, as a retired detective." Eddy kept his tone polite.

"No thanks. We have plenty of officers who are active. Besides, this is a suicide. Cut and dry."

"Are you sure about that?" Eddy frowned. "I don't mean to question you, I just wonder if maybe you're moving a little fast."

The officer shook his head. "Listen to me, there's no reason not to rush. Some guy decided to off himself and hold up everyone's train. He left a note in his room at least to keep things simple. There's no reason not to move on from all of this. The only problem I have with this case, is the two of you not following my direct orders to get back on the train."

Eddy looked over at Peter and nodded. Peter frowned but turned and walked towards the train. Eddy fell into step beside him. "What are you doing here, Peter?" Eddy locked eyes with him.

"What do you mean?" Peter tilted his head to the side.

"I mean, what are you doing on this train? Are you working a case?"

"If I was I wouldn't be able to tell you that, you know that." Peter crossed his arms and studied Eddy. "I know it's in your nature to be suspicious, but what's the real problem here, Eddy?"

"I noticed the way you snubbed me in the dining car. What was that about?" Eddy shifted from one foot to the other.

"It was crowded, Eddy. I don't like crowds. I found an open spot and stayed put." Peter sighed and shook his head. "I think you need to find a hobby, you're a bit too paranoid in your old age."

"So, you're telling me that you're not working a case? You have your nose in all of this for no reason?" Eddy squinted.

"I'm telling you that if I was, I wouldn't be able to tell you, and you should know enough to leave that alone."

"I think you should know me well enough to know that I won't. And what is your problem with Samantha?"

"I don't have a problem with her." Peter looked away.

"Listen to me, Peter. I'm not one to get in the middle of another man's personal business. But Samantha is a very good friend of mine. So, whatever your intentions may be..."

"I don't have any intentions," Peter snapped out his words. "I don't have time for this, Eddy."

Eddy watched as Peter walked away. He could tell that the man had a lot more to say, but he held it back. Eddy pursed his lips as he forced down a surge of unease. Something wasn't right with Peter Wilks, of that he had no doubt.

***

Eddy's mind flipped through the information that he knew as he walked back to the room. He opened the door and slipped inside.

"Eddy, we saw you out there with Peter and

81

the police, what is going on?" Samantha frowned.

"I saw Peter out there so I figured he might have some information."

"Did he?" Jo met his eyes.

"Yes, he did. The victim was Ryan Barker and apparently he left a suicide note in his room."

"That's terrible." Samantha frowned.

"But I know that he didn't commit suicide!" Eddy exclaimed.

"You know that for sure?" Walt asked. "How?"

"I overheard him in the dining car. He was a young man on his way to propose to the love of his life." Eddy shook his head. "There's no way he would kill himself."

"But he left a note." Jo pointed out. "Why would he do that?"

"The only time I ever saw a suicide that wasn't a suicide, it was a murder," Eddy said.

"You think that someone made it look like a suicide?" Samantha's eyes widened. "That is quite a plan to come up with whilst we've been on the train. To think it through, make a plan, and execute it?"

"It would be a stretch, but it's possible, we've already been on the train for quite a few hours." Eddy cleared his throat. "But, I think that if this wasn't a suicide, if it was a murder, someone boarded this train with the intent to kill."

"Now, wait a minute." Jo sighed. "Are you so bored on the train that you're having to invent a murder?"

"I'm not inventing anything," Eddy said.

"Sure you are. You have a young man, who left a suicide note, and then killed himself. That's cut and dry," Jo said.

"But he didn't kill himself." Eddy turned to face her.

"Because you say so?" Jo shook her head. "You don't have anything to support that."

"He was going to meet his girlfriend and propose to her." Eddy shoved his hands into his pockets in frustration. "A man doesn't kill himself just before he asks someone to marry them."

"You don't know that. You don't know what was going on in Ryan's head. Maybe he realized he didn't love her. Maybe he found out she didn't want to marry him. Or maybe he just swung into a bout of depression and convinced himself he wasn't worthy of her. All of those things are very possible. You can't just decide that someone didn't commit suicide after they've left a note," Walt said.

"My instincts tell me he didn't!" Eddy said firmly.

"Wait, why was Pete out there?" Samantha looked towards the window.

"I'm not sure." Eddy shook his head. "That's the other thing. He's acting odd. This whole situation seems off."

"Well, there's nothing normal about someone jumping off a train." Jo sighed and sank back down onto the bed. "Poor kid."

"Kid is right. He was very young." Eddy frowned. "Awfully young to kill himself."

"Suicide doesn't discriminate." Walt looked up at Eddy. "Actually adolescents and young adults have the highest prevalence of suicide. In fact, suicide is the second leading cause of death in fifteen to twenty-four year olds. I'm sorry, Eddy, but the numbers don't lie. Suicides in this country outnumber homicides five to three. The numbers say this was a suicide, as does the suicide note."

"But my gut disagrees." Eddy shook his head.

"Your gut is also full of free beer." Jo pointed out.

"Excuse me?" Eddy cut his eyes sharply in Jo's direction. "Are you accusing me of being drunk?"

"I didn't say that." Jo shrugged. "But if you think you might be, I understand, that was the point of the trip right? The free drinks and food?"

"Jo." Samantha moved between the two, which meant that she was squeezed between them because of the small space. "I think we all just need to cool off. This came as a shock to all of us. Whether it was a suicide or a murder, it's sad, and it's changed our trip."

"Yes, there's no way we can go back to just having fun." Walt sighed. "We're going to have to figure this out."

"But there's nothing to figure out." Jo shook her head. "I think that it would be intrusive to investigate."

"Jo, you didn't see this man, you didn't hear the way that he talked about his girlfriend. Leila was her name. He wanted to marry her, when a man loves like that, nothing stops him."

"Unless she doesn't love him back." Jo looked at Samantha. "Heartbreak can be too much to take."

"All right, all right. So we have an argument for suicide, and evidence for suicide. But I for one trust Eddy's instincts. So, what could it hurt if we checked things out a bit?" Samantha asked. "The train still hasn't moved, and we still have a long time before we reach our destination. What could it hurt to just follow Eddy's hunch and see where it leads?"

"You just want an excuse to talk to Peter again." Jo shook her head.

"Jo, really?" Samantha sighed.

"All right, I'm sorry. I'm just frustrated. I thought this was going to be a fun, relaxing trip. Now, it feels like it's getting out of hand."

"It's okay, Jo." Eddy glanced towards the window. "I got my feathers ruffled by Peter and the locals. I didn't mean to be so harsh. This is your trip, if you want me to drop it I will." He looked back at Jo. "I mean it."

Jo's expression softened. "You'd really stop the investigation for me?"

"I didn't say I would like it."

Jo nodded. She looked over at Walt and then to Samantha. "I guess we don't have anything better to do. Do we know where he left the train?"

"Apparently, from the rear viewing platform,

but I don't even think the doors have been roped off. The locals just want this over with," Eddy said.

"Well, let's take a look." Walt nodded.

The intercom crackled to life.

"Attention, passengers the dining car will be open to serve dinner. Please remain either in the dining car or in your room. We should be moving again within the hour." The intercom shut back off.

"Smart move, if people get hungry and cranky on this crowded train there's going to be a real problem." Eddy snapped his fingers. "All right, this is what I think we should do. Walt and I will check out the viewing platform. Jo, you and Sam can go to the dining car to see if there's any chatter about Ryan or what happened. Does that sound good?"

"Yes, we'll see what we can find out," Samantha said.

Chapter Six

Walt and Eddy walked down the corridor away from the dining car. They had to dodge the flow of people that walked towards the dining car.

"We better make this quick or the train staff are going to spot us." Walt frowned. "I don't want to get thrown off the train."

"Don't worry, it won't take long." Eddy opened the door to the back platform of the train. "I doubt he was here for long."

"What do you think he was doing here in the first place?" Walt looked around the outdoor platform. It was already getting dark.

"Well, if we assume that it wasn't to kill himself, then the killer had to be here, too. Maybe he was just looking at the view? Maybe the killer lured him somehow?" Eddy glanced through the door along the corridor. "There are plenty of rooms nearby."

"We should figure out which one was his. Do

you smell that?" Walt sniffed the air.

"What is it?" Eddy sniffed as well.

"Cigarettes. No one's allowed to smoke on the train."

"Do you think Ryan came here to smoke?" Eddy crouched down and searched the floor. "I don't see any ash or cigarette butts."

"So, maybe Ryan comes here to look at the view. Maybe he came here to smoke. He's nervous about proposing, he's trying to calm his nerves." Walt tapped his chin. "Such a dirty habit."

"Oh, so alcoholics you're okay with but smokers not so much?"

"It's just so smelly." Walt shuddered.

"If he fell off the train that doesn't explain the suicide note." Eddy frowned.

"Right, but at least we know Ryan was here. Maybe he was smoking, probably relaxed, and not expecting anyone to catch him." Walt swept his gaze towards the corridor again.

"Most people were in their rooms. But maybe

someone was following him or came across him here." Eddy narrowed his eyes. "Someone had it in for Ryan."

"Probably." Walt studied the door frame. "If those cops were worth anything they would have dusted the railing for prints."

"Yes, I agree they should have, but really, any passenger on the train could have been at the viewing platform at any time, so fingerprints might not help much even if we find them."

"What's this?" Walt pointed to a piece of red cloth caught on the railing. Eddy leaned close.

"Maybe it's someone's clothes. Do you have a tissue, Walt?"

"Here." Walt handed him a tissue. Eddy used it to tug the piece of cloth free.

"It could be from anyone." Eddy studied it.

"Do you remember what Ryan was wearing?"

Eddy closed his eyes. He remembered being in the dining car. Ryan had caught his attention because he stood out from the rest of the crowd.

He was talking very enthusiastically and his shirt was bright red.

"He was wearing a bright red shirt. It could be this color." Eddy wrapped up the tissue and handed it to Walt. Walt tucked it carefully into his shirt pocket.

"If that's the case, then maybe Ryan fought back." Walt pointed to the position of the latch. "If it was a clean shove, then the shirt never would have come near this latch."

"Whoever pushed him, fought with him to do it." Eddy nodded and stood up again. "I really think that this indicates that there was a struggle and he was murdered."

"By someone who knew enough to follow him, and to write a suicide note," Walt said. "The note was found in Ryan's room. That means that whoever it was knew which room Ryan was in."

"We need to get a look inside of that room."

***

Samantha and Jo stepped into the dining car.

It was packed, with no tables available.

"I guess the announcement drew everyone out." Samantha nodded her head towards the bar. "There's a few seats left up there."

The two weaved through the thick crowd of people. Samantha perched on the first bar stool, Jo took the next. The woman behind the counter ran back and forth as she tried to put together everyone's orders. Samantha tuned into the chatter right away.

"I heard there was a body on the tracks." A man muttered to another man beside him. "Or there was. If the train hit the poor sap, there won't be much left of him now."

"Phil, please don't be so gruesome." The man beside him toyed with his glass. "It's a horrible thing to picture."

"You're right." Phil finished his beer.

"It wasn't a body on the tracks," a woman who walked up to the bar volunteered. "Someone jumped."

Samantha listened closer.

"Are you sure? Someone jumped off a moving train? How do you know that?"

"I overheard the security guards talking about it. Apparently it's the first suicide they've dealt with." She ordered her drink and then looked at the two men. "It's too bad we all have to be delayed because of some guy's poor choice."

"It's terrible that anyone would think that was their only way out." The man who fiddled with his drink sighed. "If only he had asked for help."

"Not everyone wants help." The woman accepted her drink from the bartender.

"Hey!" A shrill voice broke through the din of conversation. "I've been waiting here forever! Where is my drink? Why did she get hers first?" Samantha leaned back on her bar stool far enough to see the woman who complained. She recognized her right away as the woman from the platform. Her speech was slurred.

"Ma'am, I told you, you have to sober up or go

back to your room. I can't serve you anymore." The bartender fixed the woman with an annoyed scowl.

"Can I at least get a drink delivered to my room like before?"

"I can't," the bartender repeated. "Please don't make me call security to escort you to your room."

"This is crazy. I just want a drink. It's not like I'm driving."

"But you are being disruptive. With everything that is going on, we don't need any added chaos in the dining car. All right?"

The woman shook her head. "No, it's not all right. I'm a paying customer just like everyone else here, and I want my drink." She slapped her hand against the bar. Samantha exchanged a look with Jo.

"All right, I'm calling security." The bartender walked towards the phone.

"No, fine. I'm leaving." She staggered away

from the bar. "No need to trouble yourself."

The bartender watched to make sure that she left. Then she turned back to her customers.

"Do you want to order something?" Jo nudged Samantha with her elbow.

"No, don't bother. It'll be too long before we're served."

"Well, it sounds like all anyone knows is that Ryan committed suicide. Maybe we should just get out of here and see what the guys found." Jo started to stand up from the stool.

"Wait a minute." Samantha spotted someone who stepped into the dining car. "Pete is here."

"Your Pete?"

"He's not my Pete." Samantha tucked her hair back behind her ears. "He's just Pete."

"Okay."

"I'm going to see if I can get his attention." She waved her hand in the air to Peter. Peter froze when he saw her. He stared with an indifferent expression, then a smile broke out across his lips.

He walked towards them.

"Samantha." He paused beside her.

"Hi Pete. This is my friend, Jo. Jo, this is Pete."

"Peter." Peter held out his hand to her. Jo took it in a firm shake.

"It's nice to meet you, Peter. I hear that you're a friend of Eddy's as well."

"Yes, we worked together in the past." Peter leaned against the bar beside Samantha. "Just like Samantha and I did." He leaned so close to Samantha that she could smell his cologne. The scent was familiar. She remembered it from the nights they had worked together. It was one of the only times she had liked the smell of a man's cologne. Her cheeks heated up as she glanced away from him.

"Sounds like you keep good company." Jo smiled. "Good luck getting a drink, there's too much of a crowd."

"Oh, I'm not interested in a drink."

"Are you working a case?" Samantha tilted her head to the side and stole a glance at Peter.

"Is there a reason you're asking?" He raised his thick, brown eyebrows. "Feeling nostalgic, Samantha?" His words were mild, but his tone was hard.

"Pete, if I did something to hurt you, it wasn't intentional." She gripped the edge of her stool as she waited for his response.

"Samantha?" He leaned a little closer and locked his eyes to hers. "Do you think this is really the place to have that conversation?"

Samantha drew back a few inches. His eyes brimmed with a strange emotion, something between anger and desperation.

"I guess not." She swallowed back her fear. "Another time, perhaps?"

"Definitely." He straightened up and looked past Samantha at Jo. "It was a pleasure to meet you."

Jo didn't answer. She only stared. Peter

started to turn away.

"Pete, wait. Do you really think this was a suicide?"

Peter looked back at her. "Eddy was sniffing around this, too. Are you investigating it?"

"I'll tell you, if you tell me." Samantha smiled.

"I'm sure the police did a fine job of looking into it." Peter rested his hand on the bar beside Samantha. "I think it's best that you leave this alone, Samantha. If you know what's good for you."

"Is that a threat?" Samantha arched an eyebrow.

"It is what it is. Ladies." He nodded to them both, then turned and pushed through the crowd.

"You had a crush on that?" Jo shook her head.

"He was much nicer back then." Samantha frowned. "He was very kind."

"Until you had your way with him." Jo poked her side.

"It's not funny, Jo. Something has definitely changed about him. It makes me wonder."

"Let's go see what the guys found. Hopefully it's more than we did." Jo stood up and started to walk away from the bar. As she moved past a man who had just retrieved his beer, she bumped into him by accident. He spilled the beer onto his shirt.

"Great!" He growled.

"I'm sorry, let me get you a napkin." Jo reached towards the bar, but the man shook his head.

"Forget it, I'm soaked. I'll have to change."

"Please, at least let me..." Jo patted the man's hands with a napkin, then froze. She noticed several scabs all over his hands.

"Skin condition," the man muttered. "I'll handle it." He turned away from Jo and left the dining car.

"You okay?" Samantha patted her arm.

"Yes. I just wish I hadn't been so clumsy."

"It's impossible not to be in here. It's only

getting more crowded. Let's get out of here."

The two women made their way out of the dining car. No one seemed to be talking about the suicide. Life had moved on for the majority of the train passengers. Once they were out of the dining car, Samantha took a deep breath.

"Phew, that's better," Samantha said.

"It was way too crowded in there."

"Excuse me, please." A staff member of the train tried to get past them into the dining car.

Samantha stepped aside. "Is something wrong?"

"Nothing. We're getting ready to start moving again, I'm just going to let the kitchen staff know."

"Wait, we're leaving now?" Jo moved closer to the man.

"Yes, in about five minutes. We've already lost a lot of time." He disappeared into the dining car. Jo and Samantha hurried back to the room. Walt and Eddy were already inside.

"The train is leaving." Jo closed the door

behind her.

"What do you mean the train is leaving?" Walt frowned. "How can they move on without the crime being solved?"

"According to them it was a suicide. They have the note. They have no reason to believe that it wasn't a suicide." Eddy shook his head. "But I'm telling you, the man that I saw today at the bar was not suicidal."

"Even if he was, death by train?" Walt shook his head. "Sure there are people who jump in front of them, or drive in front of them, but that's actually pretty rare. To jump off a train? Why would anyone do that?"

"I'm sure it's been done in the past. This can't be the first time," Samantha said.

"Of course not, but that doesn't mean that it's a common thing. There are so many other simpler ways to kill yourself." Walt sat back on the bed and frowned. "There's nothing to explain the piece of material we found."

"It could be from another red shirt or any other red clothes even." Eddy rubbed his chin.

"What red material do you mean?" Samantha leaned up against the wall of the room.

"In the railing on the viewing platform, there was a piece of red material." Walt pulled the tissue out of his pocket.

"Ryan was wearing a bright red shirt when I saw him in the dining car." Eddy pointed to the piece of cloth. "To the best of my recollection it is the same shade."

"Did you tell the police?" Samantha looked up from the scrap of shirt. "They could check to see if there's a tear in Ryan's shirt."

"A tear?" Eddy looked at her. "After jumping off a moving train down a mountain onto rocks?"

Samantha grimaced. "Good point."

"It's true though. It doesn't make much sense. I can't believe the local police were satisfied with that note." Jo sighed. "But what can we do? The train is going to be leaving in five minutes, and we're going to leave the crime scene far behind."

"Actually." Eddy swept his gaze towards the corridor. "That's not true. If we're right, and Ryan didn't commit suicide, then he was pushed or thrown from the train. If that's the case, the real crime scene is this train."

"And the murderer is probably on this train." Samantha stood up from the wall. "We're going to be on a train with a killer."

"Great. Just great." Jo shook her head. "I just wanted to have a nice weekend."

"What's nicer than an investigation?" Eddy smiled.

"It's exciting isn't it?" Samantha piped up. "I mean, not that someone is dead, but that we have a chance to figure out the crime."

Jo looked at Walt and shook her head. "Can you believe that we associate with these two?"

"It's a rather risky association. They're very likely going to get us killed one day. I've checked the numbers."

"I need some time to get some things straight in my head. Let's take a few minutes, then we'll get back together and figure out our next step. All right?" Eddy looked from Jo to Samantha.

"Sure." Samantha nodded.

As Eddy and Walt left the room, Jo and Samantha settled into silence. There wasn't much to be said.

Samantha stared out the window. The view of the mountains was astounding, but not as beautiful as it once had been. A sadness crept through the beauty.

"Do you think what Eddy said was true? Do you think Ryan was in love?" Samantha gazed out the window. "I wonder if she will ever even know that he was on his way to propose."

"I don't know about love. But if the way Eddy described it was true, I could see it as possible."

"I'm sorry about your trip, Jo." Samantha turned towards her friend. "But at least we'll still make the flower show."

"I am still looking forward to it. If we ever get there."

Chapter Seven

When Eddy and Walt made their way back to their room, Eddy's attention was drawn by someone calling his name.

"Eddy!"

Eddy looked up to see Peter. He jogged towards him.

"What is it, Peter?" He glanced at Walt. "Walt, this is my old friend, Peter. Peter, this is my friend, Walt."

"Good to meet you." Peter nodded at Walt. "Listen, I wanted to catch you because I talked to Samantha in the dining car."

"You did? She didn't mention it."

Peter looked at him for a moment. "I just wanted to warn you that getting involved in all of this is a bad idea."

"You seem just as involved as we are. Aren't you?" Eddy folded his arms.

"Eddy, trust me on this one. There's nothing to it."

"So, you think it was a suicide?" Eddy tipped his head to the side.

"I've seen the note. There's no question about it. The man killed himself, and though it's sad, it's nothing to dwell on."

"Why would it be so dangerous to get involved in investigating a suicide?" Eddy's forehead wrinkled as his brows knitted together. "What aren't you telling me, Peter?"

"Like I said, there's nothing to tell. I'd just hate to see you pull Samantha into all of this, just for old time's sake."

Walt took a step back and looked between the two men. He shifted uncomfortably as the tension grew thick. "We should be on our way, Eddy."

"You think I'm pulling Samantha into this?" Eddy laughed. "Then you don't know Samantha at all."

"Not as well as you do, it seems." Peter's jaw

locked. Eddy's lips parted with mild shock.

"Peter, there's nothing between Samantha and me. But more importantly, there's nothing between you and her either." He narrowed his eyes.

"Did she tell you that?" Peter's eyes twitched.

"She doesn't have to tell me. It's been years. Don't you think if she still held a candle for you she would have found a way to contact you? Have you forgotten that she's one of the best crime journalists around? She could have found you if she wanted to, Peter."

"Sounds to me like you're jealous." Peter smiled.

"Sounds to me like you're nuts," Eddy snapped. "I thought we were friends, but if you can't let this go, Peter, you're going to have a real problem."

"Is that so, Eddy?" Peter straightened his shoulders. "I suppose you think you're being a hero and protecting your friend from me? Well, I think the best way you can protect her is to stay out of this."

"You can leave Samantha's wellbeing to me." Eddy moved past him towards the room. "Come on, Walt, there's nothing more to say."

Walt eyed Peter as he moved past him as well.

"You're making a mistake, Eddy. You have no idea what's going on here."

"And you do?" Eddy looked over his shoulder. "If you know so much then maybe you should clue me in, or the police? If not, then I can only assume you're involved. In which case, I would advise you to stay away from Samantha."

"You would advise?" Peter smirked and shook his head. "We'll see about that." He turned on his heel and walked away.

"Pleasant friend." Walt narrowed his eyes.

"I don't know that I can call him that anymore." Eddy stepped into the room.

***

"What's bugging you?" Jo sat down on the

seat beside Samantha in their room.

"How do you know something is bugging me?" Samantha looked over at her.

"You're flicking your nails. You only do that when you're annoyed." Samantha looked down at her hands and noticed that she was flicking her nails against each other.

"Oh sorry." She let her hand rest. "It's just Pete's behavior in the dining car. It's strange. Then there's Ryan. How are we ever going to solve his murder? We have absolutely nothing to go on."

"Something will come up. That's the thing about murder, something always comes up. Eventually there is no way to hide what has been done, and who did it."

"You're right, but we don't have 'eventually' we only have a couple of hours until we get to the station. How are we going to figure it all out?" She gripped the edge of the seat and frowned. "Do you think I'm just reading too much into it, or is it possible that Pete is somehow connected with all of this?"

"Why would you think that?"

"He's on the same train as Ryan, to go to a flower show? The Pete I knew would not be bothered with a flower show." She chuckled. "I could easily believe that he was on this train to work an investigation of some kind. Then he was down talking to the police before Eddy even got to them. Why would he be so interested?"

"Ugh, for the same morbid reason that Eddy was. Those police types can't look away from a dead body."

"Maybe." Samantha tapped her palm lightly against her knee. "I can't help but wonder if he might have had something to do with Ryan."

"What would a private investigator want with some lovesick kid?"

"That's what we need to find out."

There was a light knock on the door. Jo stood up and opened it.

"Sorry, I know it hasn't been very long, but we

think we've worked out what our next move should be," Eddy said.

"Oh?" Jo stepped aside so that Eddy and Walt could squeeze their way inside.

"We need to find out what was going on in Ryan's life. In order to do that we're going to have to get to know him better. The only way we can do that, is by getting into his room."

"But wouldn't the police have taken everything?" Samantha asked.

"Probably, but they believe it was a suicide so it's still worth taking a look in case something was left behind," Eddy said.

"Well, if we want to see in his room, that's easy enough to make happen." Jo twiddled her fingers lightly against the curve of her hip.

"Are you offering?" Eddy turned to look at her.

"In the interest of not missing my flower show? Yes." She smiled.

"It's risky." Walt frowned. "There's a very

good chance of being caught. It's not like you can climb out a window or hide under the bed. The room is tiny and the corridor is long. It'll be easy enough for someone to see you breaking into the room, and even easier to see you stepping out."

"Then we'll have to create a diversion." Samantha looked over at Walt. "You and I can come up with something I'm sure. Jo can go in the room and Eddy can be the lookout." She turned her attention to Jo. "What do you think?"

"I think it could work. I guess if we're going to get thrown off the train we might as well go out with a bang." Jo walked towards the room door.

"Just remember our goal is not to get thrown off." Walt followed after her. Samantha started after him, but Eddy caught her by the forearm before she could get out the door.

"Samantha, can I talk to you for a minute?" Eddy asked. She paused and glanced at him. From how tight his jaw was she guessed it was important.

"We'll catch up, guys," Samantha said.

"Okay, we'll scope out the situation," Jo said as she walked with Walt towards Ryan's room.

"Close the door." Eddy released her arm. Samantha closed the door.

"What is it, Eddy?"

"Listen, I want you to tell me the truth about Peter. Was there something between you?"

"Why do you want to know?" Samantha narrowed her eyes. "That's a pretty personal question."

"I know it is. It makes me uncomfortable to ask, but I feel I need to." He held her gaze. "So?"

"There was nothing between us. We worked closely on the story. He provided me with invaluable information. I was grateful. We shared a few meals, maybe he saw them as dates, I saw them as having to eat while working on a story. I honestly did not mean to ignore his calls, I'm not sure how that happened." She shrugged. "That's all there was to it, nothing more, nothing less."

"How about you? Did you have feelings for

him?" Eddy continued to study her.

"What does it matter?" Samantha frowned.

"Sam, I'm not trying to pry. It's just that Peter being here on this train, it seems odd to me. His behavior has been a little suspicious. If he tries to connect with you, I just want you to be careful."

"You don't think that he could really be involved in all of this, do you?" Samantha stared at him. She trusted Eddy's instincts. If he made the same connection she started to make, she was sure there was something to be suspicious about.

"I don't know what to think to be honest. But I want you to be cautious, all right? He seems to be fixated on you."

"Really? Do you think so?" Samantha smiled a little.

"Samantha." Eddy rolled his eyes. "It might not be in a good way."

"Oh, I know, I'm sorry. But the Pete I knew would never do anything to hurt me."

"It's been a long time, Sam, and people do

change. Just let me know if he does anything that makes you feel uncomfortable. All right?"

"All right, I will." She nodded.

"If you see him in the dining car it's probably best to avoid him."

"Sure." She smiled. Samantha had no intention of avoiding Peter. Eddy's suspicions only made her even more curious about what Peter might be up to. The only way to find out the truth was to ask. Eddy opened the door and moved back to allow her to step through first. Samantha stepped out and almost knocked right into Jo. "Jo? What are you doing, I thought you were with Walt?" Samantha narrowed her eyes. It seemed to her that Jo was positioned to listen through the door.

"I was, but he sent me back here to find you. You two took longer than we expected. We found Ryan's room. It's in the next train car."

"Let's go have a look and then we'll figure out the next step." Samantha fell into step beside her. Eddy followed after her. The train rocked a little as it rolled down the tracks. Samantha looked over her shoulder at Eddy. His brows were pinched and his lips pursed. He was thinking about something. As they approached Ryan's room, Samantha caught sight of Walt. He discreetly pointed to a room that she presumed was Ryan's. Near the door of the room a woman stood. It took her a moment, then she recognized her as the drunken woman from the platform. She moved back and forth in front of the door of Ryan's room. Her eyes darted wildly up and down the corridor as if she was waiting for someone. Samantha turned all the way around to see if anyone approached from behind her. She was stunned to see Peter at the entrance of the train car, headed in their direction.

"Eddy, Pete is behind us," Samantha hissed to him.

Eddy looked over his shoulder and nodded. "Keep walking, don't stop at Ryan's room."

As they approached the room, the woman who stood outside the door, became more agitated. She paced back and forth once more, then walked into the next train car. Samantha glanced back over her shoulder again. Peter was nowhere to be seen.

"He's gone, Eddy."

Eddy paused and scanned the corridor. "Maybe he is staying in one of these rooms."

"Maybe." Samantha eyed the door to Ryan's room. "But I wonder why that woman was outside Ryan's door."

"The important thing is that she is gone now." Eddy gestured to the door. "Let's have a look."

Walt joined them. The four looked at the door with interest.

"It will be easy to get in." Jo kept her voice low. "But getting out is what concerns me."

"Don't worry, we'll make sure that no one gets down this corridor." Samantha smiled.

"How are we going to do that?" Walt wrung his hands. "I don't know what kind of diversion to create."

"Trust me, we can handle it." Samantha hooked her arm around his. "Let's go." Samantha and Walt walked down the corridor.

"Everything's clear right now." Eddy watched the other end of the corridor.

"Better now than never." Jo slid a card in the gap between the door and the door frame. With two sharp wiggles, the door swung open.

"Wow, real secure." Eddy laughed.

"I'm not complaining." Jo slipped inside. "Keep an eye out, Eddy, I'm counting on you."

"Don't worry, I have your back, Jo." He pulled the door closed.

Jo swept her gaze over the tiny room. Then she moved everything she could. It didn't even appear that the police had done a search. There was no sign of any disarray. Whatever luggage Ryan might have had was gone, most likely taken to give to his next of kin. She picked up the pillow on his bed. A ribbon fluttered out from under it. When she crouched down to pick it up she noticed that it was a hair ribbon. While she looked at it, her hand rested slightly under the bed. When she went to stand up her hand bumped into something soft. She pulled it out from under the bed. It was an undershirt.

On the tag of the undershirt four letters were printed: FBSP

It wasn't a brand name that she was familiar with. The undershirt was fairly well worn and she guessed that it was Ryan's. She looked around the room for anything else that might give her a clue as to who killed Ryan. As she was about to leave the room she noticed a brochure sticking up in the small trashcan.

She leaned down to pluck it out. Just then she heard Eddy rap on the door.

"Hurry it up, Jo."

Jo snatched the brochure out of the garbage and tucked it into her pocket. She opened the door to the room just as an angry voice filled the corridor. "You there! You don't belong there!"

Jo's eyes widened.

***

Samantha and Walt lingered near the door to the next car.

"So, what's your plan?" Walt began to pace.

"Don't worry, Walt, I'll let you know when it's time."

"But Samantha, I don't like surprises. I'd rather be prepared."

"If no one shows up, then we'll be just fine." Samantha shrugged. She watched the corridor for any sign of the train staff. Walt continued to pace. His attention shifted to the door between the cars, then to the corridor, then to Samantha. "If you keep it up you're going to wear a hole in the carpet, Walt." She shook her head. Then she took a sharp breath. "Uh oh, we're on."

"Huh?" Walt peered down the corridor. A train staff member walked towards them at a brisk pace. Samantha turned towards Walt, her eyes wide.

"We have to fight, okay?"

"Fight?" Walt shook his head. "I can't fight with you, Samantha."

"It's not like you have to hit me, you just have to say mean things."

"No. I won't. I'm a gentleman."

"Well, maybe if you'd been that way when I met your mother, things would have turned out better!" Samantha raised her voice loud enough for the man to hear.

"My mother? Why would you bring her into this?" Walt took a step towards her. "You know she's not well."

"She shouldn't be after raising a son like you!" Samantha stomped her foot. The man in the corridor slowed down.

"Samantha! What a terrible thing to say!" Walt's eyes widened. "My mother is quite proud of me I'll have you know."

Samantha lowered her voice, "I didn't mean it, Walt, it's the diversion. I'm pretending."

"Pretending or not it's still an awful thing to say." He scowled. "I think you should remember your manners."

"You there! You don't belong there!" The staff member walked towards them. "Get away from that door!"

Samantha's heart raced. She had to do something to keep him from going further down the corridor.

"You can't tell us where to be." She turned towards him.

"Oh, yes I can. I think you both need to come with me." The man crossed his arms. Samantha moved between Walt and the man.

"We're just having a conversation." Samantha shrugged.

"That conversation needs to take place in the privacy of your room. I will not stand for chaos in the corridor. We've had enough tragedy on this trip."

"It's not like I'm going to throw him off the

train." Samantha frowned.

"From the way you're talking to him, I thought you might."

"Nonsense. We're just having a little tiff. Isn't that right, Walty?" She batted her eyes at Walt. Walt's face grew pale.

"Uh yes. She doesn't like my mother."

"Look, I'm not here to do relationship counseling, take it to your room." The man started to move past them. Samantha caught sight of Jo out of the corner of her eye. She was in the middle of stepping out of Ryan's room.

"I can prove there's no hard feelings!" She grabbed Walt's face and planted a kiss on his lips. Walt's arms swung around in wild circles. "See?" She released him.

"Ma'am, that needs to happen in your room, too." The staff member shook his head in disgust. He continued down the corridor. He walked right past Jo and Eddy who walked casually towards Walt and Samantha. Walt stared, motionless, at

Samantha.

"That was close." Jo looked over her shoulder at the man who moved onto the next car of the train.

"Walt, you okay?" Eddy waved a hand in front of Walt's face.

"Walt, I'm sorry, I didn't know what else to do." Samantha couldn't bring herself to look at him. Walt shifted his gaze to Eddy.

"What's wrong?" Eddy looked between the two.

"You didn't see?" Samantha looked at Eddy.

"She kissed me. Right on the lips!" Walt exclaimed. "Samantha, I told you I don't like surprises."

"You what?" Eddy turned to face Samantha. "You kissed him?"

"I didn't know what else to do!" Samantha sighed. "The staff member was about to walk into Jo walking out of Ryan's room."

"All right, all right. The important thing is

that it worked." Eddy turned to Jo. "Was it worth it? Did you find anything?"

"Just an old undershirt, and a brochure." Jo pulled it out of her pocket. "It's for the flower show, of course."

"Wait, why would he have a brochure for the flower show? He wasn't going to the show. He was going to propose to his girlfriend." Eddy took the brochure from her. He opened it up and searched through the pages. Then he spotted something. "Someone wrote a phone number on here."

"He was picking up women on the way to propose to his girlfriend?" Samantha stifled a laugh. "So much for true love, I guess."

"A phone number doesn't mean he was picking up women. Maybe the brochure wasn't even his. It could have been left in the trash," Eddy said.

"There's one good way to find out." Samantha pulled out her cell phone. She started to dial the number. "I forgot, no reception. We'll have to wait until we get into the station."

"What about the undershirt?" Walt nodded towards the bundle of cloth in Jo's hand. "Anything to that?"

"It's just got some letters on the label, nothing else. FBSP."

"FBSP." Walt closed his eyes. "An acronym?"

"What does it matter?" Eddy frowned. "It's obviously just a clothing company. Why don't we all get some rest? We can't make any progress now until we get into the station in the morning."

"Agreed." Samantha yawned. "I could use a little sleep." She looked over at Walt. "I'm sorry again."

"A kiss, it's nothing to apologize for." He smiled.

Chapter Eight

Once Samantha and Jo were back in their room and had converted the two seats into a second bed, they went to bed. Samantha found she couldn't fall asleep.

"Jo, are you still awake?"

"Yup." She rolled over on the small bed. "How am I supposed to sleep after what you did?"

"What I did?" Samantha sat up.

"You kissed Walt! Did you see his face? I think you traumatized him." Jo laughed. Samantha's laughter blended with hers.

"I bet he used a whole bottle of antibacterial wipes."

"You think? I think he might have liked it." Jo giggled.

"What do you think about Ryan? Who do you think killed him?"

"I don't know what to think. He just seems

like a kid, on his way to propose to his girlfriend. Really, we know nothing else about him."

"So, who would have it out for him?"

"Well, I don't know, but the more I think about it I think maybe there's more to this. If he's so in love with this girl, why is she such a long train trip away from him? Why weren't they living closer together if they were dating?"

"I didn't think about that." Jo nodded in the dim light. "That's a good point. There are some people that maintain long distance relationships though."

"It's something to think about." Samantha yawned. "All right, I'm going to try to sleep again. We have a big day when we get there."

"Sure, with the investigation."

"No, I meant the flower show."

"Do you think we'll still go?" Jo peered over at her.

"Jo, I promise you, no matter what happens, we're not missing that flower show."

"Thanks Samantha." Jo sighed and turned back over to sleep.

***

Eddy gritted his teeth and did his best to remain patient. Rooming with Walt was akin to rooming with a fussy infant.

"No, sorry that's too bright." Walt sighed.

Eddy turned the light down. "How's that?"

"No, sorry it's too low."

"Why don't you do it?" Eddy grunted.

"I can't. I've already put my foot cream on. I can't walk until it dries." Walt pulled his blanket up to his chin. "Just a little brighter and it will be perfect. Thanks Eddy."

Eddy sighed and inched the light up. "How's that?"

Walt tilted his head back and forth on his pillow. "It'll have to do I guess."

Eddy plopped down on his bed. "I still can't believe you kissed her."

"She kissed me," Walt huffed. "It was very unexpected."

"I bet." Eddy chuckled. "Well, at least it kept us from getting thrown off the train. That was a very close call. When we reach our destination I can run down the information on Ryan and see what his history is. Maybe that will give us a clue as to who might have gone after him."

"The only problem is, once we're off the train, that means the killer is, too."

"Maybe, but everyone on this train had to buy a ticket. I'll see if I can get the passenger list. Then you can go through it."

"Sure." Walt cleared his throat. "I can do that."

"I really think we're the only ones fighting for this kid. I hope that we can figure something out and fast. I want to make sure that his death isn't swept under the rug so that the train company can save face." He rolled his hands into fists and knocked them together once. "Pow, you're dead. Sorry about your luck, your ticket has been punched."

"I'm sure they care more than that. But to the untrained eye, this is a suicide."

"I guess." Eddy settled back in the bed. He closed his eyes. Silence filled the room. "I still can't believe you kissed her."

"She kissed me!"

"But you let her."

"Well, I am a gentleman, after all."

Eddy laughed and tried to focus on sleep. There would be a lot of leg work to do when they arrived.

It seemed to him that he had just closed his eyes when the crackle of the intercom woke him.

"We will be arriving at the station in thirty minutes. Please take time to make sure that you have collected all of your possessions."

Eddy sat up in his bed. His mind was groggy as he tried to focus. Walt sat across from him on his bed. He rested his hand on his bag and stared at Eddy.

"Do you want me to pack for you?" Walt asked. "I've already had a shower so you can quickly have one."

Eddy forced himself out of bed and wiped at his eyes. "Did we even sleep?"

"Oh yes. Well, you did. Eddy, I think you may need to see a doctor."

"Huh? Why?" Eddy stood up and stretched.

"There's the snoring."

"What?"

"Really, I'm concerned about your health."

"My health? You can't even open a door without washing your hands."

"True. But I am in perfect health." Walt stood up.

"Good point." Eddy yawned.

"I'll just have a quick shower."

After showering Eddy returned to the room.

He found Walt had already packed everything up for him.

"Thanks," Eddy said as he tossed the items he used in the shower into his bag. "We'd better check in with the girls and make sure that they're awake."

Walt opened the door and nearly walked into Samantha. "Oh Sam, hello." He stepped back.

"Don't worry, Walt, I'm not going to kiss you." She laughed. "We just came to see if you two were awake."

"All set." Walt patted his bag.

"I need some coffee." Eddy yawned and stepped out of the room behind Walt.

"I think we all do. It's still early enough. Why don't we stop for breakfast before the flower show? We can make all of our phone calls and do some more research before we go. Is that okay with you, Jo?"

"Sounds perfect."

Eddy slid the strap of his bag over his shoulder, then he took Samantha's bag. Walt took Jo's. The four walked towards the front of the train. As they moved through the crowded corridor, Samantha caught sight of a man who jabbed his finger repeatedly at his cell phone. She paused beside him.

"Is there reception yet?"

He looked up at her then looked back down at his phone. He turned his back to her without saying a word. Samantha was left a little flustered by how rude the man was, but she was soon swept along with the crowd. There was a bit of a wait to get off the train as everyone tried to exit at once. Samantha could hear the chatter of people around her.

"Can't believe that poor kid committed suicide."

"It's so sad, he had so much life left to live."

"I'm sure it's not that big of a loss." Those words drew Samantha's attention. She turned towards the voice to find it belonged to a man who offered a lopsided smile to her. She stared at him as he reached up to scratch his cheek. His hand was covered in scabs. She remembered him as the man who Jo spilt her drink over. Samantha was about to say something to him, but the line began to move. Eddy looked back over his shoulder to make sure that she was following him. Samantha lost sight of the man in the crowd. She didn't think much of it, she knew some people were more detached from tragedy than others.

As they filed off the train Samantha noticed Peter near the security guard. She was tempted to go over to him. She had to get away from Eddy first, or he would never let the conversation happen. She pulled Jo aside.

"Pete's over there."

"Do you think he knows something more than we do?" Jo asked as she spotted him as well.

"I think I'm going to find out."

"Do you want me to go with you?" Jo looked at her with concern.

"No, it's fine. I want to talk to him myself. I need you to distract Eddy for me."

Jo glanced over at Eddy. He was trying to

keep Walt from wiping his hands again.

"All right, but if you need me, I'm just a phone call away. I'll have Eddy help me see about a cab."

Samantha nodded. Jo walked over to Eddy and Walt.

"Boys, it's going to be hard, but we have to get a cab to give us a ride." Jo pointed to the long line of passengers from the train that were waiting for a cab.

"That will take forever. I'm going to make some calls to see what information I can get about Ryan." Eddy pulled out his phone.

"I'm going to find a restroom to scrub my hands in." Walt shuddered. "I had to hold onto the railing to get off the train."

Samantha waited until Eddy's back was to her, then she walked towards Peter. He appeared to be in a heated discussion with a security guard from the train. Peter nodded and the security guard walked away from him. Samantha paused just behind him. When he turned around he took a sharp breath of air at the sight of her. "Samantha, I didn't expect to see you again. Didn't Eddy scare you off?"

"I'm not one to take orders." Samantha tipped her chin upward and looked into Peter's eyes. "What were you talking to the security guard about?"

"Nothing important." He returned her gaze, his own eyes wide open. "What is important is what I can do for you."

"For me?" Samantha shrugged. "I just wanted the chance to say goodbye. I guess we didn't get that last time."

"No, we didn't." His eyes darkened. "You really don't remember, do you?"

"I'm not sure what you expect me to remember. All I know for certain was that once we were working on a case together, we had a good time, we solved a crime, and now there seems to be a problem between us. I honestly don't know what I did to upset you."

"On the night of the arrests, I asked you to meet me for coffee the next day. I planned to ask you on a real date. You agreed, but you never bothered to show. Then you ignored all of my calls and e-mails."

"Oh Pete, I probably didn't even hear the question. If I was about to break a story wide open that was probably what I was focused on. Nothing else would have gotten through to me. I'm sorry that you felt slighted, but it was not intentional."

"Then I guess that fate has given us a second chance. Maybe now, we can have that cup of coffee."

"Maybe, if you tell me why you were on the train in the first place."

"I told you, I'm going to the flower show."

"I don't believe you." She shook her head. "It might have been years, but I know you better than that, Pete."

"Samantha. I would love the opportunity to get to know you again. I really would. But I'm telling you right now that if you don't let this go, you're going to regret it." He held her gaze with his own. "Not just you, but all of your friends, too."

"Pete, are you trying to threaten me?" She stared at him in shock.

"No. It's not a threat, Samantha. It's a warning. I want you to know that I respect you, and Eddy, but if you can't keep your noses out of this then we are going to have a problem."

"Why are you concerned about a young man who committed suicide? What do you get out of all of this?"

"I could ask the same of you." He straightened his shoulders.

Samantha met his eyes with bold determination. "Well Peter, I happen to be interested because I do not believe that he committed suicide. I believe he was murdered."

"Samantha!" Peter glared at her. "You need to take a step back from this and fast. You don't understand what's happened here. You just don't."

"If you do, then you need to tell me. What has happened, Peter?" She looked straight into his eyes. "If you know so much and think I know so little, then tell me the truth."

"You probably think that I'm being cruel, Samantha, or seeking some kind of revenge. But that's not the case. Walk away from this, just go with your friends and enjoy the flower show."

Samantha stared at him a moment longer. His expression was rigid. She didn't think she'd get another word out of him. She spun on her heel and walked away from him, back towards Jo. Eddy looked over at her just in time to see Peter walk away.

"Did he try to talk to you, Samantha?" Eddy asked when he caught up to her.

"It doesn't matter," Samantha avoided his gaze. "I want to go enjoy the flower show."

"I found out some very interesting

information. Our pal, Ryan, the young and promising husband-to-be, just got out of jail, Free Bank State Prison," Eddy said as Walt joined them.

"FBSP," Walt said with recognition. "The acronym on his shirt."

"I think they supply their own clothing to the prisoners usually, don't they?" Samantha asked.

"Some do." Jo nodded.

"What crime was he in for?" Samantha's mood perked up.

"Fraud. Apparently, Ryan was involved in one of those get rich quick schemes, you know the pyramid type. Well, people lost a lot of money to him, and he went to jail for two years for it," Eddy said.

"Huh, so Ryan gets out of jail, and gets on a train to go to propose to his girlfriend. What if she rejected him?" Jo asked.

"What do you mean? He didn't even have the chance to ask." Samantha shrugged.

"That we saw," Eddy said.

"What do you mean?" Samantha asked again.

"He could have called her and proposed. Maybe when she turned him down, he didn't want to live anymore. Maybe the piece of material in the railing wasn't even from his shirt." Eddy frowned.

"No, Eddy that's not possible," Samantha said.

"Just because we want to see a murder here, Samantha, maybe we were wrong. Now that I know Ryan was a recently released criminal, it changes things. He was probably going through the elation of being free, and thinking that he was going to have the perfect life. Then his girl turns him down, he's crushed, he's a little drunk. Maybe he jumped, maybe he fell."

"Eddy wait, that's not why it's impossible. It's impossible because he couldn't have called his girlfriend. I tried many times and there was no reception on the train. How could he have called her?"

Eddy raised an eyebrow. "I'm sure there was a way. Maybe he just happened to try when there was reception or maybe he e-mailed her."

"There was no internet either, besides I doubt a guy like that is going to e-mail his proposal, he was determined. He would want to at least hear her voice."

"You may be right, I'm not one to know much about the matters of the heart. What I do know is that Ryan is not the good kid we thought he was. He might have some enemies on the train."

"Good thought," Samantha said. A cab rolled to a stop in front of the four. Eddy reached out to open the door for Samantha, but before she could get inside Eddy caught her eye.

"Remember what I said about Peter. I've got a bad feeling about him."

Samantha searched his eyes. "I will." She slid into the cab.

Chapter Nine

The ride to the coffee shop was a short one. It was located right beside the entrance of the flower show. While Jo and Walt ordered, Eddy and Samantha set up shop at a corner table.

"We know that Ryan did his time at Free Bank State Prison." Samantha pulled out a notebook and opened it up on the table.

"Unfortunately, I don't have any contacts there to find out much about him. It's a little out of my reach," Eddy explained.

"Well, lucky for us nothing is out of my reach." Samantha smiled. "I just need a few minutes and we'll know what Ryan ate for breakfast and when he took his naps."

"Really?" Eddy raised an eyebrow. "I must say your contacts are impressive, Samantha."

"It comes from years of begging, threatening and in some cases bribing people to help me on stories, Eddy. I don't think there's a prison that I don't have a contact in."

"I guess that's something that you should take pride in."

"It's going to get us our answers, right?" She began dialing a number on her phone. While she talked on the phone, Jo and Walt joined them at the table with coffee and muffins.

"That smells so good." Eddy took one of the cups of coffee as Samantha hung up the phone.

"Okay, so this is what I found out. Ryan was let out early for good behavior. He was a model prisoner with no disciplinary issues."

"So basically, nothing?" Eddy frowned. "This guy isn't giving us a clue to go on is he?"

"Well, not nothing. I did find out the address he gave when he entered the prison system. It's not far from here."

"So, I guess we should go there." Jo sipped her coffee.

"No way, you are not missing the flower show." Samantha took her cup of coffee and looked at Jo across the top of it.

"I think a murder investigation is a little more important than a flower show." Jo took a bite of her muffin.

"I agree." Eddy narrowed his eyes. "The longer we wait to follow this up the more likely that any information we could find will be gone."

"That's great. So, you and Walt can get a cab and go check the address out, while Jo and I go to the flower show."

"Oh." Eddy shrugged. "That's fine with me. Walt?"

"Sure." Walt picked at the wrapper on his muffin.

"Won't you guys be disappointed to miss the flower show?" Jo frowned.

"Uh, no." Eddy grinned. "Not at all."

After they finished their breakfast the four stood outside the coffee shop to finalize their plans.

"Okay we will make sure that we keep in

touch." Samantha checked her phone to be sure that her ringer was on.

"I'll let you know if I find out anything." Eddy tucked his phone into his pocket. "Just remember that whoever the killer is, might be at the flower show. Keep your eyes open."

"We will." Jo smiled. "Let's go, before we miss the first exhibit."

Samantha waved to Eddy and Walt then followed after Jo to the entrance of the flower show.

***

"All right, Walt, let's track down this address and find a cab."

"Not another one. If I get home without contracting some disease I will be amazed."

Eddy smiled at Walt. "Normally, I think you're overreacting a little when it comes to the germ thing, but cabs are one thing I can agree with you on." He stuck his hand out to hail a cab. As he looked towards the road he saw Peter on the sidewalk. He was walking towards the entrance of the flower show. "Maybe we should stay with the girls." Eddy started to lower his hand just as a cab pulled up next to the sidewalk.

"Eddy, Samantha and Jo can handle themselves. It will only offend Samantha if you keep hovering over her."

"Oh, you know so much about women now?" Eddy frowned.

"I don't know about women, but I know that Samantha is a fully capable, intelligent, experienced woman who will have no trouble navigating the likes of Peter Wilks. Now, let's do our part and let them enjoy their flower show." Walt sat down in the cab. Eddy looked towards the entrance of the flower show once more, then slid into the cab beside Walt. He stared out the window as the cab rolled away from the flower show. He hoped it wasn't a mistake to leave Samantha alone with Peter.

Walt gave the address to the driver.

"That's a short ride." The driver started to pull

away from the curb. Walt sneezed right behind the driver.

"Oh wow, really? Do you think you could cover your nose? I don't want to be exposed to your germs!"

Walt's eyes widened. Eddy tried not to laugh.

"I'm sorry, it was unexpected, of course. I have a wipe if you'd like one."

"That's all right, just keep your germs to yourself."

The ride to the address was short, just long enough for Eddy to send a text to Samantha.

Peter is at the flower show, use caution.

When they reached the address she had not responded yet.

Eddy put his phone away and then stepped out of the cab. He handed the driver the payment then turned towards the house. There were two cars in the driveway of the small rancher. The yard was tended and the house had a fresh coat of paint on it.

"Do you think it's his parents' place?" Walt studied the house.

"I'm not sure. I didn't check into who owns it. I guess we're about to find out."

"Do you want me to wait?" the driver asked.

"No, but I'll give you a call so you can pick us up if you're still in the area when we need you."

The driver nodded and handed him a card. Once the cab pulled away Eddy and Walt headed up to the front door of the house. Eddy checked his phone one last time and then knocked on the door. The door swung open to reveal a petite young woman with a smile on her pink lips. Eddy didn't know what exactly to expect, but this was not it.

Eddy and Walt introduced themselves. "We're looking for information about a man who used to live here," Eddy said.

"Do you mean Ryan?" She narrowed her eyes.

"Yes, how do you know him?" Eddy asked as Walt looked past her into the house. He could see that it was very neat. He also noticed boots at the back door, and a baseball cap hung on a hook on the wall. He doubted they belonged to the small woman before him.

"Look, I already know he's dead. The cops were here to inform me because he never changed his address with the prison system. So, if you got your wires crossed and think you need to tell me again, don't bother."

"That's not exactly why we're here." Eddy slid his hands into his pockets. The woman was obviously not broken up over Ryan's death, but he wanted to know who Ryan was to her. "We'd like to know if you can tell us anything about your brother."

"My brother?" She laughed. "He wasn't my brother. He was some stalker who wouldn't take no for an answer, and the only thing that I can tell you about him is that I'm glad he's dead. He did us all a favor by taking care of the problem himself. So, if you expect me to shed a tear, you've come to the wrong place."

Eddy leveled his eyes on hers. "So, you must have been his girlfriend?"

"I was not his girlfriend. We dated for a little while, then he got arrested. I would never be with a criminal. I had no idea what he was up to. The cops questioned me up and down because they thought I was involved, but I wasn't. Ryan got it in his head that he could scam rich, old ladies for millions, and he did. When I met him he was rolling in cash and claimed it was honest money. When he went to jail he started sending me letters and trying to call me all the time. I told him I didn't want anything to do with him. He sent me letters saying that he couldn't live without me, and that he would make sure we were together. Honestly, the freak scared me." She lowered her eyes for a moment. "When I heard he was getting released, I was afraid he was going to show up here and do something to hurt me. Then he called and left a message the day before yesterday saying he was getting the train and going to come see me. He acted as if I should be excited."

"So, you had no feelings for him at all?" Walt raised an eyebrow.

"Only hatred. He kept interfering in my life, even from jail. He found out about Cory." She looked over into the living room as a tall, burly man walked into it. "Who is my fiancé, and he tried to cause me trouble by sending Cory letters. He wrote these horrible things about how I was cheating on him with Cory and that when he got out of jail he would make it clear who I belonged to. Like I'm some kind of object. I'm a person, you know?"

Walt's gaze fixated on the man that stood a few steps away from Leila.

"Of course. Well, the reason we wanted to ask you some questions is because there's some concern that Ryan did not commit suicide," Eddy said.

"What do you mean?" Her eyes widened.

"I mean, there is some evidence to support the fact that he might have been murdered."

The woman's face drained of color. She looked over at Cory. Then she started to close the door. "I don't want to answer any more questions. You guys aren't even cops, are you?" She pushed the door closed. Eddy knocked again, but she did not answer. He could hear the two arguing inside the house, but he couldn't make out what they said.

"Well, she's a real sweetheart." Eddy shook his head. "Sounds like Ryan was a little off his rocker."

"Eddy, that man in the house, he was on the train."

"What?" Eddy looked at Walt. "Are you sure?"

"Yes, I'm sure. He had scabs all over his hands. Remember? He was picking them on the platform. I won't forget that for years."

"So, Cory was on the train with Ryan." Eddy smiled a little. "Sounds like this may turn out to be a bit of a love triangle."

"If Cory knew it was a murder it didn't look like he told his fiancée about it, though. She was shocked to hear it might not have been suicide." Walt tapped his finger against his hip. "I think we're going to need more than just the two of them being on the train together to prove this."

Chapter Ten

The flower show was in full swing by the time Samantha and Jo got there. Samantha wiped the back of her hand across her forehead. It wasn't too hot, but the sun was bright and she sweated easily.

"Why don't I get us some lemonade?" Jo pointed out a vendor cart. "You look like you could use something to cool you off."

"Sure, that would be great." Samantha leaned against a railing that surrounded one of the exhibits. As she scanned the crowd she thought about the text Eddy had sent. He saw Peter enter the flower show. So, where was he? She and Jo had been to a few of the exhibits. She did one more sweep of the crowd, then caught sight of the woman that had dropped her suitcase on the platform. She stood in front of someone and appeared to be quite upset. Her shoulders shook, her hands flailed, and she shifted from one foot to the other. She remembered seeing her rather upset outside Ryan's room before they searched it. Was she just always drunk and upset?

Samantha shook her head and started to look away when the man she spoke to stepped to the side. Right away she recognized Peter. He stared at the woman with a stern expression and poked one finger into the palm of his opposite hand as he spoke. To Samantha it looked like he was explaining something, or trying to get his point across. The woman shook her head and turned away from him. Peter turned and walked away from her. For a moment Samantha considered going after him, but now she was more curious about the woman. Why was she talking to Peter? She recalled that when the woman stood in front of Ryan's room Peter walked down the corridor towards her. Was his intention to meet with her then? Samantha walked across the path to the woman.

"Excuse me, my name is Samantha. I noticed you talking to that man. Is he upsetting you?" Samantha offered the woman a tissue.

"No, it's not him. I'm Sandra Banks. That

name used to mean something." She accepted the tissue and dabbed at her eyes. "He's only tried to help, but I fear things are beyond help now."

"What do you mean?" Samantha studied her.

"I know you look at me, and all you see is a drunk loser. You should have seen me five years ago." She sniffled. "I had everything. I made a lot of money, I married a man I thought I could trust, and I thought I was set for the rest of my life. Instead, I had everything stolen from me. Every last penny." She rubbed the tissue under her eyes.

"That's terrible," Samantha sympathized.

"I thought, he would pay, the man who took everything from me. But he didn't. He got out free to live his life and be happy. He never had to suffer the consequences. While I am ruined."

"I'm sorry that happened to you, but surely there's some way to improve your situation. There's always the chance to start over."

"No, not now I'm afraid. Now it is far too late." She sighed and looked at Samantha. "I can see that life has given you plenty to believe in. But for me, life has taken everything. I don't have hope anymore. Look, I'm even prepared to speak to strangers about it. There's no hope for me."

"Is there someone you could talk to about the way that you're feeling?" Samantha leaned closer to her. "You shouldn't be alone like this."

"Maybe not. But I am. Don't worry, I have no intention of doing myself harm. I am not that brave." She blew her nose and wadded up the tissue. "Please, don't waste another thought on me. My time has come and gone, you still have time left." She turned around and walked away from Samantha. Samantha considered following her, but she knew that the woman didn't want to talk anymore. Her mind focused on one tiny detail that the woman said. She believed the man who had stolen from her was going to pay. Was it possible that she meant Ryan?

"Here you go, one ice cold lemonade." Jo held the drink out to her. Samantha accepted it with a smile.

"Thanks Jo."

"Were you talking to that woman again?"

"I was. I need to make a quick phone call, Jo, is that okay? I can meet you at the next section."

"All right." Jo's gaze lingered on her. "Anything I can do to help?"

"No, I just want to check something with Eddy."

As she walked towards the next exhibit, Samantha pulled out her phone. She dialed Eddy's number.

"How are things blooming?"

Samantha was startled by Eddy's question. She broke into a smile. "How clever. I wish I could say beautifully, but I have a question for you."

"Shoot."

"When you found out the information about Ryan did it include the name of his victim?"

"Yes, it did."

"What was it?"

"Give me a second. Yes, here it is. Sandra Banks was the victim. There were others but she took the largest hit and also drew her friends into the scheme with him. At first the police considered that she might be involved in the crime, but when they saw she had invested nearly all of her fortune into the scheme they no longer suspected her."

"I think we might just have our killer. The woman on the train who was standing near Ryan's room before we broke into it is Sandra Banks."

"That's great, Samantha, but wait..."

"And there's more. I just saw her talking to Peter, I think he must be connected to her, and perhaps he is the one who pushed Ryan off the train..." She paused and winced. "Though I hate to think that he would do such a thing. At least we now have a good idea of who the killer is."

"Samantha, that is very interesting, but we believe we found the killer."

"What?" Samantha gripped the phone tighter.

"We went to the address you gave us and it is the home of the girl who Ryan was going to propose to. Only, she wasn't interested in Ryan at all, he was obsessed with her. We met her fiancé, Cory, who just happened to be on the train with us. We're pretty sure he's the one who pushed Ryan off the train."

"If Cory was on the train and Sandra was on the train, I hate to say it Eddy but I think we have two suspects."

"Well, Cory is certainly big enough to have pushed Ryan off the train. Let's not forget that Ryan was young and muscular, he'd probably been working out while in prison. The cloth on the railing indicates that he did most likely struggle, so there isn't much chance that the woman I saw on the train would be able to overpower him."

Samantha frowned. "I know. Which is what led me to the suspicion that perhaps Peter is branching out from his private investigation activities into murder for hire."

"Wow." Eddy cleared his throat. "I guess we

can't be sure. I'd hate to think that about him, too."

"It would explain why he keeps trying to scare us off the case."

"I guess the only thing we can do is follow both leads and see how they pan out. Right now Walt is looking up information about Cory to confirm he purchased a ticket for the train, so we can have proof."

"I can make some calls about Peter. I think it's pretty clear that Sandra Banks had an ax to grind, and we know that she was on the train. I want to confirm that she hired Peter. We need to see if we can find evidence to prove that Peter was involved."

"Involved in what exactly?" The voice came from just behind her. Samantha's chest tightened.

"Eddy, I have to go."

"Is something wrong?"

"I'll call you soon." She hung up the phone. Then she turned to face Peter. "What are you doing here?"

"I'm here for a flower show. As I walked by I happened to hear you mention my name a few times. So, what is so interesting about me, Samantha?" He held her gaze. "You weren't that interested before."

"Maybe meeting Sandra Banks made me more interested."

"Who?"

"Don't play innocent with me. I saw you talking to her. I know that you are working for her."

Peter stepped closer and looked into her eyes. "What exactly is it that you think you know, Samantha?"

"Pete, I've thought you were capable of a lot of things, being a great cop, being a good friend, but never has it crossed my mind that you might be involved in a murder."

"Murder?" Peter took a slight step back. "Do you really want to throw around accusations like that?"

"What am I supposed to think? You won't tell me the truth. I know that Ryan is the one who caused your client to lose her fortune. She must have been beside herself with anger that he was let out early." Samantha tilted her head to the side and studied his features. "Was it that you felt so much sympathy for her and you knew it would just be getting rid of a criminal? Do you think that just because it's been ruled a suicide, you're going to get away with it?"

"You have no idea what you're talking about. I was wrong about you all those years ago, and now I'm wrong about you again. You never really had a clue about me, did you?"

"I'm not interested in a walk down memory lane, Peter. I just want to know the truth." A small crowd of people walked past them. Their chatter momentarily silenced their conversation.

When they passed, Peter replied, "Samantha, if you really thought I was a killer, I don't think you'd be standing here in front of me. If you want to spread accusations about me, that's your choice. But leave my client out of it."

"So, you admit that she hired you?" Samantha smiled briefly.

"I'm not saying another word." Peter spun on his heel and disappeared into the crowd.

***

Eddy stared at the phone with his brows knitted close together.

"What is it?" Walt eyed him. "Is something wrong?"

"I'm not sure. It's not like Samantha to just rush me off the phone like that." He tapped his phone against his palm, then looked up at Walt. "We'd better get back to the flower show. If Peter is there, and Samantha suspects him as much as she does, they are bound to run into each other."

"That won't be good." Walt shook his head.

"I've got the list from Chris of who bought the tickets," Eddy said as he handed Walt his phone. Chris was a young lab tech that used to work with

Eddy at the police station. He had proved himself to be an invaluable contact and friend. "On the way let's see if we can confirm that Cory was on the train. Also, find out anything you can about a passenger named Sandra Banks."

Walt nodded and looked at Eddy's phone. The drive back to the flower show was a quiet one. Eddy hoped that Samantha was safe. He knew that she tended to be much more daring than she should be.

Chapter Eleven

When Eddy and Walt arrived at the flower show, Jo and Samantha waited near the entrance.

"Did you find out anything more?" Samantha frowned.

"No. What about you? Why did you have to get me off the phone so fast?" Eddy raised an eyebrow. Samantha considered telling him about her encounter with Peter, but she didn't want to. Not just yet. She wanted to find out a little more information before she revealed her true suspicions.

"There was this beautiful flower on display and I didn't want to miss it."

"Oh?" Eddy said skeptically. "Was it a cactus?"

"Oh hush." Samantha frowned. "Let's get some lunch and regroup."

The four gathered around a picnic table with an assortment of food purchased from a nearby food truck. Walt ignored his sandwich as he shared what he had discovered.

"I just looked through the ticket and passenger list and Cory Smith did indeed purchase a ticket. However, I found something interesting. Another ticket was purchased only a few hours later by a Mick Smith."

"Well, Smith is a very common last name. Do you think it connects to anything?" Samantha took a bite of her meatball sub.

"The thing is that the tickets were purchased on the same day a few hours apart. They were also purchased for the same connecting train. That seems like a bit too much of a coincidence to me." Walt tried not to look at the sauce that dripped down Samantha's chin.

"Maybe, but it is still a common name. Samantha, could you find out if there's a connection between Cory Smith and Mick Smith?" Eddy asked.

"I can. After I'm done eating." She took another bite. Walt looked away and thrust a napkin in her direction. She took it and rolled her eyes.

"Some food is meant to be messy, Walt."

"There's something bothering me about this whole thing." Jo ignored her chicken salad sandwich.

"What is it?" Eddy looked over at her.

"So, we know that Ryan was on his way to propose. We also know that he was on the same train as the woman he went to jail for defrauding. What are the chances of that? I can understand that Cory bought a ticket when he found out that Ryan was getting out, but what about Sandra? Did she just happen to be on the same train as Ryan?"

"You think she knew about Ryan's release, too?" Samantha's eyes widened.

"It would make sense." Eddy nodded. "Usually the victim is notified if the offender is going to be released, especially if it's an early release."

"So, Sandra found out about Ryan getting out

and she decided to hop on the train?" Eddy rested an elbow against the picnic table. "Sounds like premeditation to me."

"I'm still not sure." Walt shook his head. "I don't think that she could have done it."

"I still think we should look into her further," Samantha said.

"I'm going to call Chris and see if we can get a copy of the suicide note. It should be on the system. Maybe the handwriting will give us a clue of some kind." Eddy frowned. "It can't hurt."

"Good idea." Samantha nodded. "I'll look into Sandra Banks."

"I'm going to eat my food." Jo grinned and took a bite of her sandwich. Eddy walked away to make his phone call. Samantha used her phone to search for information about Sandra Banks. It was pretty easy to find considering that she was a well-known name in high society at one time. She didn't work, but inherited her fortune from her family.

"Would you believe Sandra was once honored for making a donation of over one million dollars to a charity?" Samantha shook her head. "She doesn't sound like someone who was bent on murder."

"Maybe not, but it's easy to be generous when you have money. Her life was defined by her wealth. She didn't seem too concerned about giving it away. That's probably why she was so easily swayed by Ryan's con. We know that Ryan took everything from her." Jo took the last bite of her sandwich. "I'm sorry, but in a way she was asking for it. If you don't know what it's like to have nothing, you don't know how vigorously you should protect your funds."

"I imagine there are some fiscally responsible people who are very wealthy." Samantha continued to flip through photographs of the woman. She froze when she came across one picture in particular.

"Actually, Jo is correct," Walt said. "There are not too many people that are very wealthy that can handle their money. Most have a team of professionals handle their finances from top to bottom. They don't even buy a pack of gum without someone knowing about it."

Samantha barely heard him as she stared at the picture on the screen.

"Is that Peter?" Eddy paused just behind Samantha and peered over her shoulder at the phone. "With Sandra?"

"Yes, it is." Samantha turned her screen off. "We already know that he's working for her."

"Hm." Eddy sat down beside her. "Chris said he didn't have time to send the suicide note through straight away as he was going to a meeting, but he had a quick look at the note on the system for me. He said the words were not surprising, but that the stationary used was quite distinctive. The paper was light green and it had the letter L as a watermark."

"Hopefully he'll send it later," Jo said.

"What's next then?" Eddy asked.

"I think we still need to look at Sandra," Jo said.

"I remember the bartender refused to continue serving Sandra drinks in her room. Maybe if I talk to the steward about the drinks he can tell us what time he delivered them," Samantha suggested. "That way we can try to piece together where Sandra was around the time Ryan died."

"That's a great idea." Eddy cleared his throat. "Samantha, I have a question for you."

"Hmm?" Samantha glanced over at him.

"Would it bother you if I looked into Peter's background? I'm curious about what he's been up to over the past few years." Eddy frowned. "If you don't want me to, I won't."

"Why would I have a problem with it?" Samantha shrugged. "It's fine with me. I'm sure if there is something there for you to find, you will find it."

Eddy held her eyes for a moment longer and

then nodded. Samantha occupied herself by calling the train company office number. She asked to speak with the steward that was on their train. She was given another number to call. She dialed the number and waited for the steward to pick up. She placed a notepad in front of her on the table. The scribbles she drew on the paper were mostly just to distract her while she waited.

"Hello, this is Thomas."

"Hi Thomas, my name is Samantha. I'm calling you because I need a favor."

"Were you a passenger on the train?"

"Yes."

"Oh. Well, how can I help you?"

"I'd like to know if you can recall serving a certain passenger drinks."

"I can't really comment on a passenger's activities," Thomas' voice was drawn out in an attempt to be authoritative.

"Thomas, I'm aiding an investigation into the unfortunate death of one of the passengers on the train."

"Yeah, that was terrible. But that was a suicide."

"That's yet to be determined."

"Really?"

"I'm not asking for much, Thomas. I'd just like to know if you actually delivered any drinks to Sandra Banks' room?" Samantha reflected actual authority in her voice. "No stone unturned you know. You don't want to be the person that impedes this investigation."

"I thought the police ruled it a suicide?"

"It's being looked into. So did you deliver drinks to her?"

"Yes, I delivered her some drinks. Not that it matters. There's no way that she had anything to do with the death."

"How can you know that for sure?" Samantha listened close as she sensed that Thomas knew much more than what he was saying.

"Hey, I could lose my job for this. I'm not

supposed to hang out in passenger's rooms. I need you to keep this off the record."

"No problem, I can do that."

"Well, when I delivered her drink she was crying. She was alone, and I felt bad for her. She was just bawling her eyes out. So, I asked her what was wrong. She couldn't really talk, so I just sat with her. I was still with her when the train stopped. There's no way she could have been involved. But like I said, I need this to stay off the record."

"I understand." Samantha made a note on her notepad and then tapped her pen against it. Just when she thought everything added up, everything fell apart. "Well, thanks for your time, Thomas."

"If anyone was involved in the death, I would think it was the guy that was sitting with Ryan in the dining car. They were really having it out."

"What guy?"

"I'm afraid I don't know his name. I just went

to the bar to pick up drinks and food to deliver to the rooms. I guess it was only about an hour before that I saw them, because I stayed in Sandra's room after that."

"What about his room number? Do you know that?"

"No sorry, I don't. But the bartender might. If he paid the tab then his room number would be on the receipt."

"Do you know how I can contact her?"

"Sure. I'll give you her number. But don't tell her I'm the one that gave it to you. She's a little funny about her personal information."

Samantha raised an eyebrow. She expected that might be because Thomas was so willing to give out her phone number. She jotted down the number that he gave her. After she hung up she caught sight of Eddy looking towards her. In an attempt to avoid another conversation about Peter she quickly dialed the bartender's number.

"Gretta, speaking."

"Hi Gretta, I'm sorry to bother you, but I'd like to ask you a quick question about something that happened in the dining car this past trip."

"Oh? How did you get this number?"

"I promise that it will only take a second. Do you remember the man who died?"

"Yes, I saw him in the bar. He was bragging about getting engaged. Tragic." Her dry tone indicated she didn't really think it was too tragic.

"Did you notice him getting into an argument with anyone while he was in the dining car?"

"Oh uh." She paused a moment. "Who is this again?"

"I just need to know if you can recall the other man's name, or room number. Then I will not bother you anymore."

"I do remember him arguing with this guy. I noticed because I've been a bartender for a lot of years, and when someone starts fighting, I look for certain things."

"Like what?"

"Like if they might be carrying a weapon, or if they are wearing heavy jewelry. The guy he was fighting with was wearing a really thick ring. I was worried that he might haul off and punch him, as crowded as the dining car was that could have started a huge fight."

Samantha made a note about the ring on her notepad. "What about a name? Did you hear any names?"

"All right. It was Rick. I think. No, like the mouse."

"Mickey?"

"Yeah, but just Mick. I think that was it."

"Thanks, you've been very helpful."

"Great, now maybe you can tell me who keeps giving out my number."

"Sorry, bad connection." Samantha hung up the phone. She knew better than to reveal her sources. "I just found out something very interesting."

She drew the attention of everyone at the

table.

"What is it?" Walt squinted at her.

"It sounds like our Mick Smith had a heated conversation with Ryan before his death. He also wore a very thick ring."

"Just like his son. Mick Smith is Cory Smith's father." Eddy tapped the screen of his phone which displayed a photograph of the two men together. Each wore an identical ring. "I took the liberty of looking it up." He winked at Samantha.

"So, then maybe Cory's father went to bat for him?" Jo suggested.

"So maybe they planned the murder together," Eddy said.

"Let's not forget that Sandra is a very viable suspect." Walt wiped his mouth with his napkin. "Where there is money trouble murder often follows."

"She would be, but Thomas, the steward, confirmed that he was with her the entire time."

"Is it possible that she bribed him?" Jo

brushed her long, black hair back over her shoulder. "It's not as if that's unheard of, people have done it to create an alibi before."

"It's possible. What's also possible is that her distant cousin took care of the problem for her." Eddy slid his phone over to Samantha. "This is what I found when I looked into Peter."

"They're related." Samantha nodded. "That still puts him in the hot seat."

"So, you're saying after all of this work we're still not any closer to finding out who the murderer is?" Walt shook his head.

"Well, we can visit our friend Cory again to see if he has anything to say about his father being on the train." Eddy finished his food.

"I think that's a good idea. But this time, can I go with you?" Jo looked at Eddy. "I want to see Cory for myself. I'm very good at telling if someone is lying."

"All right." Eddy nodded. "It would be good to go and speak to him with someone else. Throw him off a bit. Give me a few minutes I want to talk to Walt about something." He wanted to tell Walt to keep a lookout for Peter.

"Sure." Jo glanced over at Samantha. "Are you going to join us?"

"No, I don't think so." Samantha tapped at the screen on her phone. "I want to do a little more checking into Pete. I think that this idea about Mick is a stretch."

"All right. Hopefully when we get the copy of the suicide note, something will stand out."

"I forgot all about that phone number on the brochure Jo found. We should give it a ring out of curiosity." She rummaged in her purse until she found the brochure.

"Good idea." Jo glanced over at the brochure which was splashed with images of the flower show. A shadow passed across her features as she looked away. Samantha frowned and pulled out her cell phone.

"I'm sorry that we're missing some of the

show. I promise that we won't miss all of it."

"It's okay. You know this is more important to me than flowers. There will be other shows."

Samantha dialed the number on the brochure. She listened to two rings before someone picked up.

"Wilks."

Samantha's hand trembled as she held the phone. Of all the people she expected might answer, Peter Wilks was not one of them. She hung up quickly.

"Samantha? Who was it? What's wrong?"

Samantha put her phone down on the table. She bit into her bottom lip. When she released it she met Jo's eyes. "Peter Wilks answered."

Before Jo could respond the phone started to ring. Samantha stared down at the phone number on the caller ID display, it was the same number that she had just dialed. "It's him."

"Don't answer it." Jo shook her head.

"But maybe I should?" Samantha picked it up

before she could convince herself not to. "Hello?"

"Samantha?" Peter sounded surprised. "I didn't know that you had this number. Why did you hang up?"

"I didn't have this number. Ryan did. Written on a flower show brochure that we found in his room. Care to explain how he got it?" She braced herself. The last thing that she expected was for Peter to tell the truth.

"I gave it to him."

The revelation made Samantha's breath catch in her throat. She didn't really want to believe that Peter could have killed Ryan, even if all the evidence pointed at him, and her own instincts screamed that he was possibly responsible.

"Why?"

"To try and befriend him so I could find out as much as I could about him. I wanted to see if there was anything I could use to put him back in jail. When Sandra hired me, she said she didn't want him walking free. I assured her that a criminal like

187

that would likely have more than one skeleton in his closet. So, I waited for the opportunity to speak to him and once I had it, I gave him the impression that I could help him clear his name. I wanted him to trust me and confide in me any other crimes he may have committed."

"And did he?"

"No. He was squeaky clean as far as I could tell. He just kept repeating the same stuff about how much he loved his girlfriend and how he was going to spend the rest of his life with her. I realized I was getting nowhere, so I jotted down my number and asked him to call me if he wanted to work on clearing his name. I hoped that he would maybe get a little drunk and decide to confess something to me. It was a last ditch effort to help Sandra. Obviously that didn't work out."

"Pete, you two are cousins aren't you?"

"Samantha, I know what you're thinking, and you're right. I would do just about anything for family. But not this. Never this."

"Are you sure? Maybe you just got upset with

him, maybe you were just trying to teach him a lesson of some kind. You didn't mean to hurt him, but he wasn't listening."

"No, that's not true at all." Peter's voice rumbled with anger. "If that's what you think of me, then there is nothing left to say." He hung up the phone. Samantha held the phone to her ear a moment longer as if she wasn't ready to put it down. She wondered if she had pushed him too far. Maybe he was innocent, in which case she definitely didn't want to antagonize or upset him.

"You okay?" Jo looked at her.

"I think so."

"Ready?" Eddy looked at Jo as he and Walt walked back over.

"Samantha and I will look into Mick from here." Walt sat back down across from Samantha. "But only after she finishes her meatball sub."

Samantha tried to smile, but her heart fluttered with an unnamed fear. If Peter really was a killer had she just given him a reason to target them all?

Chapter Twelve

The silence in the cab as Eddy and Jo rode to Cory's house was thick.

"So, have you seen any groundbreaking flowers?"

Jo looked over at him. "I've seen some beautiful ones."

"Groundbreaking, you get it, because flowers grow out of the ground." Eddy gave a short, awkward laugh.

"Oh, clever." Jo spared a small smile. "I get it."

"I'm sorry this is interfering with your vacation."

"It's all right, it wouldn't feel like my day was complete without investigating someone or something." Jo looked out the window at the passing trees. "It's a good thing that you're here or it would just be me and Samantha looking into the murder. That could have been messy."

"What's going on with her? She seems distracted."

"On the contrary, she is highly focused."

"Huh?" Eddy frowned. "She's barely said a word about Mick."

"That's because she doesn't think Mick is the killer. She's focused on Peter, she thinks he's involved."

"Oh." The cab lurched to a stop outside of Leila's house. "I can understand why she would think that. Once we rule out Mick, I'm likely to agree with her on that opinion," Eddy said thoughtfully.

"You think he's guilty, too?"

"I think he may not be guilty of murder, but I think he's guilty of something. He must have been on the train to do something, it's just too much of a coincidence. There's Cory." Eddy looked down the driveway.

Cory's large frame made its way towards the end of the driveway weighted down by a large trash bag. "Thanks for the lift." Eddy slipped the driver payment, then he nodded to Jo. Eddy grabbed the handle of the door and eased it open. Jo did the same on the passenger side. With muffled footsteps they approached Cory, who dropped the large bag of trash into the trashcan. Jo moved behind him and Eddy blocked his path back to the house.

"Hi there, Cory. Remember me?" Eddy smiled.

"What do you want?" Cory glanced over his shoulder at Jo. His gaze lingered on her for a moment, then he turned back to Eddy. "What's this about?"

"It's about the fact that you were on a train yesterday with your fiancée's ex. Did she know that you threw him off? Did she ask you to do it?" Eddy narrowed his eyes.

"I don't know what you're talking about."

"There's no point in lying, Cory, we know that you were on that train. We have an eyewitness that can place you there, not to mention that you bought a ticket in your own name. Not a great idea if you're planning to commit murder. But you thought that everyone would assume it was a suicide. You'd be free and clear. I guess you weren't counting on this," Eddy said. Cory glared at him. He pursed his lips and then shook his head.

"All right, I was on the train, but that doesn't prove anything. I didn't even speak to Ryan. I spent most of the trip in my room trying to get the nerve up to confront him. I wanted to protect Leila, but to be honest with you I didn't want to get into a fight. I was going to confront him, but I kept delaying it and then before I could he was dead." He grimaced. "Now you've got Leila thinking I had something to do with his murder. But I didn't. No matter what anyone says you can't prove that I did, because I didn't." He glared into Eddy's eyes. "You can believe whatever it is you need to, but it won't change the facts. I was on that train to talk to Ryan, to get him to leave Leila alone, that was it. I didn't even do that."

"Why not? Don't you care about Leila?" Eddy stepped around the trashcan towards him. "You're going to marry her, but you can't come to her defense?"

"Look." Cory frowned and leaned one hand against the trashcan lid. "Because of my size everybody thinks I'm tough. But the truth is, I don't like confronting people." He sighed. "I didn't want to look like I was too weak to protect her so I offered to go get on the train and prevent him from coming here. I would have, too, but obviously, I didn't have to. He was dead before the train arrived."

"Or maybe you did and this is the best cover story that you could come up with. Hmm?" Eddy crossed his arms. "I'm not buying it. I bet you confronted him and things went from bad to worse. Maybe it was a fight that just got out of hand, maybe it wasn't your fault." Eddy pressed, trying to sympathize with him so he would confess.

"Look, it wasn't me. I didn't even talk to him.

I did overhear someone else talking about him though." He nodded his head. "And that lady was angry."

"What lady?" Eddy narrowed his eyes with interest.

"I don't know her name. She was pretty drunk. I heard her arguing with this guy in the corridor. He kept saying that she had to let it go, he hadn't found anything they could use. She told him that Ryan was worthless and that he had to pay for what he did. She said, if he couldn't find a way to make him pay, then she would have to." He shook his head. "I just figured she was another person he had crossed. From the way they were talking though, it seemed like Ryan had done a lot more harm than just stalking. I figured if they were already gunning for him I didn't really need to jump in. I guess I was right."

"I don't know what makes you think that you can get away with trying to pin this on some woman." Eddy laughed. "Ryan was far larger than her."

"Then you know who I'm talking about?" Cory

raised an eyebrow. "You know who the woman is?"

Eddy grimaced. He had let too much slip. He tried to use it to his advantage. "Sure, I've already ruled her out as the killer. Anyone else you want to try to frame?"

"Look, I'm not framing anybody. If you cleared her then I guess she didn't do it, but I can tell you, I wouldn't want her to be my enemy. She was fierce and drunk. Have you ever tried to fight with a drunk woman? Even if she's small, I bet she can pack a punch. Look, I've got to get back inside before Leila notices that I'm gone. She's pretty upset about all of this. It took a lot to convince her that I had nothing to do with his death. If she sees me talking to you, she might not believe me anymore."

"I'm not sure that I believe you." Eddy lifted the brim of his fedora and wiped away some sweat that had gathered there. "I can tell you that we will be in touch."

"Whatever." Cory shook his head. "I had nothing to do with it, so you're not going to find anything on me."

As he turned and walked back inside, Jo faced Eddy. "What do you think? Is he lying?"

"It's hard to tell. But I do think it's time we had a conversation with this woman that he defrauded. It sounds like she had a very big score to settle. She's so small though." He began to walk back towards the car. Jo let him get a few steps ahead of her. Then with a burst of speed she ran up to him from behind. She had his arm twisted behind his back and his body thrust forward before he could even think to struggle.

"Bam, you're off the train, Eddy. Her size wouldn't have stopped her if she took him by surprise."

Eddy cleared his throat and started to resist her grasp. She only tightened her grip. "Jo, let me go."

"Oh, I'm sorry, I thought we were still acting out the idea." She released him and took a step back in case he decided to retaliate. "But do you think she could do it now?"

"Absolutely, but you're a lot stronger than she

is and it just seems very unlikely." Eddy shot her a sullen look as he ran his hand along the reddened skin of his wrist. "Or at the very least I know not to get on anymore trains with you."

"As long as you're good to me, you have nothing to worry about." She cast him a quick wink.

"I'll keep that in mind."

As the two walked back towards the street Eddy cast a glance over his shoulder. He caught sight of Leila peering out through the curtains of the front window. When she saw him turn, the curtains fell shut. Eddy called a cab which arrived within a minute. Once they were back in the cab Jo looked over at Eddy.

"Why didn't you mention Mick?"

"I wasn't ready to. Not yet. I don't want Cory to know what we know until we learn a little bit more about Mick. If we tip them off then they will do their best to get their stories straight. I want to know that I can get a confession out of him before I move forward with any accusations."

"Your mind amazes me sometimes." Jo

smiled at him.

"Why?" Eddy rubbed his forehead. "Lately it seems to be failing me more and more." Jo was surprised that Eddy was so open with her.

"You don't just see what's right in front of you, you see the whole story. You think about past, present, future, and all the ways a person has created connections throughout their lives. I guess that's what made you a great detective."

"Did you just say great and detective in the same sentence?" Eddy arched a brow as he looked over at her.

"It's a compliment, old man, just enjoy it."

"Fine, I think I will." Eddy looked over at the window, but Jo still caught sight of the slight curl of his lips into a smile.

Chapter Thirteen

Jo and Eddy returned to the café where Walt and Samantha were waiting for them.

"It took me a little time to sort through all of the Mick Smith's, but I think I have it narrowed down to the same man that purchased a ticket on the train. I have confirmed that he is Cory's father. It has just been the two of them since Cory's mother died in a car accident ten years ago. There are no records of remarriage. From what I can tell Mick's not rich, but he's comfortable." Walt frowned. "He is a businessman and there's nothing to indicate that he would take such a large risk as to kill someone."

"Maybe not as a businessman, but as a father." Samantha flipped through the photographs on her phone. "I found some old articles in the local paper about Cory winning some wrestling competitions, his father is by his side in every picture. It seems like the two are very close. Maybe Mick is protective of him."

"Maybe. Or maybe he got on that train with Cory to try to stop him from taking Ryan's life. He just didn't get the chance." Walt frowned. "With Cory's experience in wrestling I'm sure that he would have no trouble getting Ryan off the train."

"Good point." Samantha nodded. Her expression darkened as her mind returned to Peter. He sounded so offended when she last spoke to him. Still, she couldn't shake the idea that he was involved. It made sense for him to be the murderer even though she hoped he wasn't. Yet, Cory was also a very likely candidate. She shook her head as her mind raced in many different directions.

"Well, we found out that Cory claims that he wanted to talk to Ryan to stop him but he never got the chance." Eddy and Jo walked up to the table.

"Oh?" Samantha looked up at him. "Did you ask him about Mick?"

"No I didn't. I wanted to wait to see what you found out first. Anything?"

"Only that Mick is a very stable man with good business sense and a deep affection for his son." Walt canted his head to the side. "Does that sound like a murderer to you?"

Eddy pulled off his fedora and ran his hand back through his thin, brown hair. "No. But people are not always what they seem. In fact they are rarely what they seem on the surface. Right Samantha?" He cast a glance in her direction.

"Right." She looked back at him without hesitation. She knew that he was trying to bait her into discussing Peter, but she was not ready to.

"So, what's our next step?" Jo did her best to break through the tension between the two. "Are we going to hunt down Mick and talk things over with him?"

"I don't want to tip him off. I think we need to talk to the police. Going to the local police station that attended the scene is not a possibility because it's too far from here. But I asked Chris, and he found out that the station that would investigate the crime if it was a suspected murder is a bit of a drive from here, but it's not too far. I don't know how much they'll know because it's being treated as a suicide, but it's worth taking a shot and seeing if they know anything. If we can get an idea of whether they found anything the slightest bit suspicious on the body then we might be able to gain some actual proof that we could use to try and get a confession out of whoever might have done this." He looked over at Samantha again.

"Okay, let's do it." Jo pulled out her phone. "I think we're making the cab service around here rich."

"No, wait a minute, there's no reason for all of us to go." Samantha stood up. "Eddy's the one with police connections and Walt has the eye for detail. You and I can finish out what's left of the flower show."

"That doesn't sound fair," Jo said.

"Oh, it's fair." Eddy grinned. "More than fair, trust me."

"I don't know, Sam, is it right to enjoy something like this when we are trying to find a murderer?"

"Nonsense, we are not going to miss out on the rest of the show."

"Are you sure?" Jo tugged at the strap of her purse. "I mean I know you enjoy an investigation, but the show only happens once a year."

"Jo, you don't have to justify it. The whole point of this trip was this show. Besides, Eddy and Walt will be hot on the trail of whoever did this. There's no reason for us not to be able to enjoy a little foliage. Right boys?" She flashed a smile in Walt and Eddy's direction.

"Absolutely." Eddy tugged his hat back down on his head. "Right Walt?"

"Right." Walt nodded. "Have fun. Try not to kill any plants, Samantha." He grinned at her.

"It was one plant!"

"One cactus." Jo grinned.

"All right, let's just go." Samantha laughed and walked towards the entrance of the flower show. Jo followed after her.

"I guess we'd better call another cab." Walt sighed.

"Are you kidding me? My wallet is almost drained. Besides, there's an easy way to get a ride." Eddy grinned at Walt.

"Huh how?"

"Well, we're going to the police station. All we need to do is get picked up by a patrol car."

"I'm not getting arrested!" Walt growled.

"I'm not talking about getting arrested." Eddy pulled out his phone. After a quick search he found the number of the police station. Then he dialed it. As soon as someone picked up he met Walt's eyes. "Hello, I'd like to report a murder."

Walt's eyes grew huge. "Eddy!" Eddy turned away and continued to speak into the phone.

"Yes, I have evidence that the man who jumped off the train, did not jump at all. He was pushed. Right, well I can't come down to the station because I don't have a car." He paused and nodded. "We're at the flower show. All right, we'll be here." He hung up the phone. "Done, and done." He grinned as he turned back to face Walt. His grin faltered when he saw how pale Walt's features were. "What?"

"Eddy, in your experience when someone claims that there's been a murder, who do you first suspect?"

"The person who reports it." Eddy shrugged.

"So, you've just made us both prime murder suspects. We were on the train, so we had the opportunity."

"But no motive." Eddy smiled. "Yes, I want them to suspect us as that's the only reason they will send a car out here to pick us up. It saves us money, plus we can gauge the officers that pick us up to see if they are going to be allies."

"Or, if they're going to lock us up for murder you mean?" Walt shook his head. "It's a bold move, Eddy. I can't say it's a bad move, but it's a bold move."

"It worked didn't it?" Eddy pointed to the

patrol car that pulled up to the sidewalk. "Our chariot awaits."

"Well, it'll probably be cleaner than a cab." Walt sighed with relief.

"Ha, if you say so." Eddy refrained from detailing the amount of drunks that had thrown up in the back of his patrol car when he worked as a police officer.

Two patrol officers got out of the car and walked towards them. "Did one of you call us?"

"We both did actually." Eddy straightened his hat. "We'd like to talk to a detective."

"What about?" The officer narrowed his eyes which were already shadowed by the brim of his hat.

"Let's discuss that at the station." Eddy smiled. "Shall we?" He opened the back door of the patrol car. The two officers looked a little put off by his forwardness, but did not stop him. Walt slid in beside him. As soon as he put his foot down on the floorboard of the back seat his pale features tinged with green.

"Eddy, there is a puddle on the floor."

"Oh yeah, last guy we picked up had a bladder problem." The officer in the passenger seat laughed. "Sorry about that."

"Bladder? Did he say bladder?" Walt looked over at Eddy with his mouth wide open.

"He's just pulling your leg." Eddy smiled. "But if I were you I would keep your feet up."

Walt did just that for the remainder of the ride to the police station.

When they arrived at the station it was much smaller than they expected. There was a general sleepy atmosphere. A few of the officers even had their feet propped up on their desks and their chairs tipped back. It was a very relaxed environment.

"Not much action around here, hmm?" Eddy glanced at the officer.

"We like it that way." He smiled. "There is the detective." He pointed to one of the men who had his feet propped up on a desk. "Detective Richardson."

The detective snorted and then opened his eyes. "What is it?"

"Are you working on the death from the train overnight?" Eddy asked.

"Why would I be?" He laughed. "A suicide doesn't need much investigation."

"Unless it wasn't a suicide." Walt offered him a friendly smile. "Did you consider that possibility?"

"Of course not, we had the suicide note, not hard to predict what happened when someone spells it out for you, is it?" He sat up in his chair and then leaned forward across his desk. "You two claim to know something, so please, educate me."

"It was clearly a murder." Walt tapped his finger lightly against his palm. "Ryan had just been released from prison, he was free, not depressed. He was on the way to claim the hand of the love of his life. He was happy. Not only that but we believe that we found a piece of his shirt on the railing by the viewing platform."

"Oh? A piece of shirt?" Detective Richardson laughed. "That seals it then. I guess we can go out and arrest someone because of a piece of shirt. Oh wait, there are no suspects, because this was not a murder. Are you two a bit senile?"

"Excuse me, Sir?" Walt narrowed his eyes. "Not only is that a very discriminatory comment, it is completely untrue. My mind is as sharp as it has always been."

"Really? Did you have a little accident there?" He pointed at the cuff of Walt's pants and his soaked shoe.

"That was the result of a disgusting puddle in the back of one of your filthy police cars. I can't believe that you would even transport criminals in that nasty environment."

"Uh huh. Well, you haven't told me anything solid here. Did either of you witness the crime?" He raised an eyebrow.

"No." Eddy began. Before he could give any other explanation the detective pushed forward.

"Did either of you commit the crime?"

"Of course not." Walt scowled.

"All right then, you have no actual knowledge of a murder being committed. Why are you wasting your time?"

"Was the crime scene even evaluated? Was any evidence gathered at all? Were there any marks on the body not caused by the fall?" Eddy asked.

"Did we examine a body that was battered by rocks after jumping off a moving train for any marks that were not caused by the fall?" Detective Richardson asked incredulously. "As for the crime scene, it was rocky terrain. There was nothing to be evaluated. We didn't collect any evidence because there was no need for it."

"What about from his room?" Eddy's eyes widened a little. "Was anything unusual found there?"

"Other than a suicide note signed by the person who committed suicide? No." He frowned. "I don't know why you've gotten it into your heads that this was a murder, but it wasn't. Now, it may have looked like I wasn't doing much when you walked in, but sleep is actually very important to me. So, if there's nothing else." He thumped one foot and then the other back up on the desk. "I'd like to get back to it."

"Sure, we shouldn't interrupt your beauty sleep with actual police work." Eddy started to turn away.

"Maybe if you had something to show me, we could talk."

"I've got two prime suspects and a hunch." Eddy shrugged. "That's all I can offer right now. I was hoping that you might have more. But I can see that you've already tabled this case."

"I've done my job. If you can bring me something that proves me wrong, please do." He closed his eyes.

Walt and Eddy exchanged a frustrated glance.

Eddy knew the detective was right. They didn't have enough to even make a case for a homicide.

"We're going to need a ride." Eddy sighed.

Chapter Fourteen

The attendance at the flower show had thinned out. Samantha strolled through the displays with Jo who snapped pictures along the way. She started to relax and really enjoy herself as she had intended to on the trip.

"This was a great idea, Jo."

Jo smiled from behind her camera. "It's easy to forget your troubles when you're surrounded by beauty."

Samantha nodded in agreement. She paused in front of a large display of purple flowers. As Samantha looked over the bright purple blossoms she felt a slight prickle along the back of her neck. She knew that there was no reason to be suspicious, but the feeling was usually a sign that someone was watching her from a distance. Her instincts rarely failed her. She decided to move along to the next exhibit and see if the feeling moved along with her. Maybe a random bug had crawled from a petal onto the back of her neck. She slapped at the exposed skin.

"Look at this." Jo pointed out a blossom that looked similar to a feather with long, white tendrils. "I think this would look very nice in my garden. What do you think?"

"Uh huh." The prickle raced along her skin again. Samantha looked over her shoulder with a sharp movement.

"Samantha? Are you okay?" Jo frowned.

"I'm sorry, Jo. I just have this weird feeling. It seems like someone might be following us."

Jo surveyed the crowd behind them. "It's pretty crowded."

"I know, but sometimes there's that sensation of being watched. I feel that now."

"Do you think it's Peter?"

Samantha bit into her bottom lip. "I don't think so. After our conversation on the phone I doubt that he's interested in speaking to me again. Besides, I'm sure he wouldn't just follow me."

"I wouldn't be too sure about that. After all we suspect he might be involved." Jo's shoulders tensed as she looked over the crowd again. "Keep your eyes open, Samantha. Not only is Peter a possible suspect, but if he didn't do it, we don't know who did. It could be anyone in this crowd."

"I hate to think that. Unless we find some serious evidence that Ryan was killed his case will remain closed." Samantha gritted her teeth. "That would be terrible."

"It would." Jo nodded. "Hopefully Eddy and Walt will come up with something."

"I'm going to use the restroom." Samantha headed towards the building that housed the restrooms. Before she could open the door the back of her neck prickled again. She felt on edge as she looked around her. There weren't too many people by the building. Samantha spotted a woman who stood only a few feet from the bathrooms. She didn't hide the fact that she was staring right at Samantha. She looked to be in her twenties and quite petite. Samantha had no idea who she was, but there was no question that she was looking straight at her.

"Is there a problem?" Samantha locked eyes with the woman.

"Yes there is. A very big one. You know, when people showed up at my door, I assumed they were connected with the police in some way, but now I know better."

"Who are you?" Samantha looked at the woman with widened eyes.

"My name is Leila, which I'm sure you already know. You and your friends are trying to ruin my life."

"Leila?" Samantha smiled a little. "Ah, now I understand. Have you been following me?"

"I just want to know why. Why is that you think you have the right to interfere in my life? Everything was fine, and then Ryan got released from prison. Now you and your friends are accusing my future husband of killing Ryan."

"It was clearly not a suicide." Samantha

folded her arms across her chest. "Doesn't that bother you at all, Leila? Your ex, who was so in love with you that he wanted to spend the rest of his life with you, was murdered."

"No!" Leila threw her hands in the air. "No, it doesn't bother me at all! I don't care if that makes me a bad person. I'm glad he's dead. I don't care how or why. He's out of my life, that's all that matters to me. He was a terrible person. I can finally start my life without him hanging over my head. I should now have a chance of happiness. Instead my fiancé is being questioned by a bunch of busybodies. I want to know what gives you the right to interfere in my life?"

"Leila, someone was murdered. Whether you liked him or not, he was still a person who did not deserve to be thrown off a train, no matter what he did."

"You don't know that, you can't know that." Leila glared. "I want you and your friends to stay away from Cory. He had nothing to do with this. He's a gentle man who could never hurt anyone."

"Is that what you think?" Samantha said. "You have no idea what a man is capable of when it comes to protecting the woman that he loves."

"No, not Cory. He loves me, I know that. But he doesn't have a vicious bone in his body. Besides, if I wanted Ryan dead, I would have taken care of it myself."

"Is that a confession?" Samantha raised an eyebrow. "You just told me that you didn't care how he died, you were just happy that he was dead. Do you stand by that statement?"

"I didn't say I was happy. I just said it was a good thing. I didn't kill him either, obviously. I wasn't on the train, I was working." Leila sighed. "If you four continue, I will press harassment charges against all of you."

"I'll keep that in mind, Leila. Are there any other ways that you would like to threaten me?"

"Samantha?" Jo walked towards them. "Are you okay?"

Leila glared at Jo and then walked away from

both of them. "Was that, Leila?" Jo stared after the woman.

"Yes, it was."

"How did she find you?"

"I think she must have followed Eddy and Walt or you and seen the four of us together."

"What did she want?"

"Let's just say that she's not too broken up over Ryan's death. She's threatened to charge us with harassment if we keep looking into his death."

"Oh really?" Jo shook her head. "I guess that she doesn't have a problem with Ryan being murdered."

"Not at all. In fact, now I'm starting to wonder if she didn't have a hand in it. I'm going to make some calls, is that okay, Jo?"

"Sure it's fine. The flower show is winding down anyway. Only about an hour left." Jo smiled. "I'm really glad that I got to see it."

Samantha excused herself to a bench that was

out of the way and began looking up information about Leila on her phone. From her social media account it was fairly easy for her to find that Leila worked at a convenience store, 'Snacks for Sunshine'. She raised an eyebrow. She thought the name of the store was unique and not something she had seen in other areas. She guessed it was a privately owned shop. Samantha decided to see if she was really working around the time of Ryan's death. She dialed the number of the convenience store.

"Snacks for Sunshine."

"Hi, I'm calling to inquire about an employee of yours. I need to know if she was the person that I had such a great experience with yesterday. Could you tell me who was working yesterday?"

"Oh sure, it was Leila. She was here all day. She had to be because the boss had off. If you want I can let her know that you called to compliment her and leave a note for the boss."

"Actually, I'd love to talk to him myself, she was just so helpful. What's his name? Maybe I could find a way to contact him myself."

"Sure. Mr. Smith. Actually, he lets us call him Mick. Mick Smith." Samantha was shocked as she recognized the name, but she tried to hide it when she spoke.

"Oh wow, what a small world. I think I know his son Cory Smith. Does Cory work there, too?" Samantha poised her pen above her paper.

"Sure, not yesterday though. He was off, too. That's why I was glad that Leila was here with me. I must have been stocking the cooler when you came by. What did she do for you? I'd love to let her know that you called. What's your name? Can I give her a message from you?"

"No thanks. I have all I need." Samantha hung up the phone before he could ask her any more questions. She frowned. Leila clearly had an alibi. It was possible that the employee would lie for her, but with Cory and Mick on the train why would she also need to be there?

Chapter Fifteen

"Can you drop us off here, please?" Eddy knocked on the screen that divided the front and back of the patrol car. The officer pulled off to the side of the road. Walt was eager to get out of the car. The officers pulled away the moment they were out.

"Not too fond of us I don't think," Walt said. "What's your plan? I know you have something in mind."

"This is where Leila lives. Right down there at the end of the street. I think it's time we told Cory what we know about his father. It's the only card we have left to play. I want to see if he will take us to him."

"All right, let's give it a shot." Walt glanced at his watch. "We have a few hours before we have to leave on the train."

"Are you ready for this?" Eddy looked over at Walt. "He's a big guy you know. When we bring his father into it, he might get physical."

"I know. I'm not worried. We want to rile him up a bit. It's the best way to get to the truth."

"Since when did you become an expert on interrogation?" Eddy laughed with surprise.

"I know things. I watch those cop shows." Walt smiled.

"Uh oh, look out. Are you going to be bad cop?" Eddy grinned and walked the rest of the length of the road.

"I'm not so sure I could pull that off, but I'd be willing to give it a try." Walt offered a smile as he followed after him. On the way up to the house the two quietly discussed their plan of action. Before they could reach the door Cory was outside.

"You two, what are you doing here again?" His anger was clear in the tone of his voice and the tension of his balled up fists.

"We need to talk to you about your father, Cory," Eddy said.

"My father?" Cory glanced over his shoulder

at the house. "If Leila sees me…"

"Leila is the least of your worries." Walt's tone became quite gruff as he took a step towards Cory." It was a sight to see the slender, diminutive man face up to the much larger, burly man. "We want to know why your father was on that train!"

Cory stared at him for a moment, then shook his head. "No, that's impossible. He wasn't on the train. He was at the store, like he always is. There's no way that he had anything to do with this."

"I think you're wrong." Walt jabbed a finger towards Cory's face. "I think you knew he was on that train, in fact, I think you asked him to be on that train. You got him to do your dirty work, didn't you, Cory? Didn't you?"

"Okay, easy." Eddy placed a hand on Walt's shoulder to calm him. "Look, Cory we're just trying to figure out what happened here. No one is accusing anyone of anything. If you think that your father wasn't on the train, then prove it. Where is he now? We'll go have a conversation with him so that we can find out the truth."

"Fine. That's a good idea." He glowered at Walt. "But I'll thank you to watch the way you talk to my father. He's a good man, and I don't want anyone disrespecting him."

Walt and Eddy exchanged a brief look, then Walt nodded. "I'll be on my best behavior."

"He should be at his place. I'll call and check. We can take my car." As he pulled out his phone to call his father, Walt leaned close to Eddy.

"Do you think it's a good idea to get in a car with him?"

"We'll be fine." Eddy shushed him as Cory hung up the phone.

"He's at home, let's go."

Eddy managed to get a reluctant Walt into the back of Cory's car. The inside of the car reeked of smoke and stale french fries. It wasn't the worst car Eddy had ever ridden in, but Walt was clearly uncomfortable. Every time Eddy looked over at him Walt's mouth was pinched tight, and it did not appear that he was breathing. As soon as the car was parked Walt popped open the door.

"Now, I want the two of you to remember that you are talking to a good man. One word out of line and I'll knock you both out, got me?" He glared at Walt and Eddy. "I'm not afraid to hit an old man."

"We're not that old. I mean, sixty is the new thirty really." Walt shook his head.

"Not the time, Walt." Eddy spoke out of the corner of his mouth.

Walt nodded and quietened down. Cory led them both into a small house. They walked down a short corridor to a door.

"This is my father's office." He knocked on the door. "Dad, are you in there?"

"Sure, come in."

Eddy looked over at Walt and nodded. Cory opened the door to reveal a small office with expensive, well-cared-for furniture. The smell of the wood polish greeted Eddy's nostrils as he stepped inside.

"Hi Cory. Who are these gentleman?" He stood up. "I'm Mick Smith." Eddy offered his hand, but Mick shook his head slightly and raised his hands to show them to Eddy. "Sorry, skin condition." Eddy noticed the scabs on his hands as well as a large ring. "Hereditary," he added as he looked at his son and cringed slightly.

"My name is Eddy, and this is my associate, Walt. We're here regarding your presence on the train yesterday, the same train where a young man met a tragic death."

"Oh." Mick lowered his hands to his sides.

"Dad, just tell them the truth." Cory shook his head and then looked back at his father. "Tell them where you were yesterday, because I know it wasn't on the train."

"Please sit." Mick sat back down in his chair and gestured to the two chairs in front of his desk.

"We have records that show you were on the train, Mr. Smith. Did you purchase a ticket?"

Eddy settled into the high-back, leather chair that faced the desk. He could feel the man's eyes as they bore into him.

"Yes actually, I did purchase a ticket. I was on the train yesterday. My intention was to scout out a location to open a new shop." He shrugged.

"Dad? You never told me about a new shop. Are you really going to open one?" Cory appeared mystified as he stared at his father. Walt's gaze fixated on the man's open briefcase on his desk.

"It was a surprise, Cory. I wanted to surprise you with it as a wedding gift. I thought you would be able to manage it yourself, and maybe Leila would work in the shop with you." He sighed and closed his eyes for a moment. As he reached his hand up to rub at his forehead Walt leaned forward in his chair and narrowed his eyes.

"Wow, Dad, that is so generous of you. Thanks." Cory's voice was softened by shock.

"I was going to tell you about it on the train," Mick said. "But the train was so busy that I never even saw you." Eddy continued to study the man before him.

"Still it seems rather convenient that you were on the same train as your son, that's a long way away to look for a shop. Did you ever meet Ryan?" Eddy asked.

"Ryan? Oh, that troublesome fellow." He shook his head. "Honestly, I only know what my son has told me about him. He seems like a terrible man."

"Did he seem that way when you were having an argument with him in the dining car?" Eddy stood up from the chair and rested his hands on the desk before him.

Mick shifted in his chair. He looked from his son back to Eddy. "So, what if I talked to him? That doesn't mean anything."

"Dad? You talked to him?"

"Cory, you have a good thing going with Leila. I knew that Ryan would be the only one that could mess that up for you. I knew that you wouldn't be able to confront him. You've got your mother's soft heart."

"Dad..."

"No, now wait, there's nothing wrong with that, Cory, nothing at all. But I couldn't just stand by and watch this criminal show up in your lives and turn everything upside down. How is that fair? You two should have been married before he got out, and instead he was let out early. That messed up everything for everyone." He sighed and reached up to rub his forehead again.

"Is that how you got those scratches?" Eddy tilted his head towards the man's wrist.

"Huh?" Mick looked at his hand. "Oh, I must have scratched it when I was getting my luggage out of the storage room."

"Doubtful," Eddy said. "Those scratches were caused by human fingernails. I can tell by the pattern and shape of the scratch."

Mick slid his hands under the desk. "I don't know what you're talking about."

Walt was still staring at the briefcase. Eddy

followed his gaze to the briefcase. He was staring at paper sticking out of it. It was light green and Eddy could see the watermark, a letter L, sticking out the top of the briefcase. Eddy looked at Walt and nodded his head slightly.

"Okay, then, how about the paper you have there in your briefcase? It has a unique watermark," Eddy said.

"What about it? Anyone can buy that stationary." He narrowed his eyes. His features grew tense. Eddy leaned a little closer.

"So, it's just a coincidence that Ryan used the very same paper to write his suicide note. I wonder if we submitted a sample of your writing for handwriting analysis, would it match the writing on the suicide note, Mick?" Eddy's voice raised with every word he spoke.

"That's enough!" Cory moved between Eddy and the desk. "This is crazy. You can't really think that my father was involved in Ryan's death."

"Well, it doesn't matter what I think, Cory. What matters is what a jury will think, when it's proven that your father wrote the suicide note, that his DNA is under Ryan's fingernails, and that he was on the train with motive at the time of the murder." Eddy didn't back down from Cory, but he did allow some room for the father and son to make eye contact. "You did it for your boy, didn't you, Mick? You did it for the right reasons."

"Dad, tell them it isn't true!"

"I did what I had to do." Mick shook his head. "But it wasn't the way you think. It was an accident."

"An accident?" Eddy pressed. "How so?"

"I saw Ryan outside on the viewing platform smoking a cigarette. I just wanted to talk to him again, to make it clear that he had to leave Leila alone. But he got angry when I tried to talk to him. He took a swing at me. I ducked it. He came for me and we scuffled a bit and then I pushed him off me. I never expected that the door in the railing would open." He grimaced. "When it swung open, Ryan fell out, it all happened so fast, I didn't even have time to try to catch him."

"Dad, don't lie. You didn't do this, I know that you didn't do this." Cory's eyes were wide and filled with tears as he stared at his father. "It's not possible."

"It was an accident." Mick stared at his own hands. They trembled as he held them out before him. "I just wanted him to listen. He was going to take everything from you. He was going to take Leila or hurt her. I couldn't let him do that. I just wanted him to understand that. I had no idea when I shoved him that the door would open. I was in shock."

"But not so much shock that you couldn't fabricate a suicide note, right?" Eddy tipped his hat. "That was some very quick thinking on your part."

"All right, I was scared. It all seemed to happen on autopilot. I wasn't even supposed to be on the train. So yes, I faked a suicide note. I'm not proud of what I did, but let's be honest, it wasn't a great loss, was it?"

"Yes." Eddy stared at the man across the desk.

"Any loss of life is a great loss. Ryan was a person, he deserved to have the chance to live his life. All you had to do was get a restraining order, Leila could have gotten one. Then the moment he came near her, he would have been back in jail. Instead you killed him, not because you wanted to protect your son, or Leila, but because he made you angry, so angry that you shoved him. You wanted to get rid of him, didn't you?"

"I didn't." Mick clenched his jaw shut tight. "Not like that."

"Dad, we need to get you a lawyer, don't say anything else." Cory moved to his father's side.

"I think we've heard plenty." Eddy turned towards the door. "We'll be on our way."

Before Eddy could reach the door, Cory stepped out in front of him.

"I'm sorry, I'm afraid I can't let you leave." He couldn't quite meet Eddy's eyes, but his massive frame did an effective job of blocking the doorway.

236

"Step aside, Cory, we are leaving." Eddy started to brush past him. Cory placed his hand on the door to prevent it from being opened.

"No. You're not." He reached into his father's desk drawer and pulled out a gun.

"Cory, what are you doing?" Mick stood up behind his desk.

"I can't let this happen, Dad. I can't let you go to prison for doing something that I should have done." Cory continued to block the door. Eddy shot a glance at Walt whose face had grown pale. The two men were not free to leave, in fact, Eddy suspected that Cory might never let them leave at all.

Chapter Sixteen

Samantha checked her phone for what felt like the hundredth time. She sighed. Jo looked up from her phone. She was looking through the pictures she took at the flower show.

"Samantha, what's wrong?"

"I am really worried. Eddy isn't picking up. It's been too long for them to just be talking to Cory. What do you think we should do?"

"Is there a way we can track their phones?" Jo frowned.

"I'm not sure. It would take a while for me to arrange that and it might be too late by then."

"We can go to Leila's house and see if Cory is there." Jo stood up. "Let's not wait another minute. Our train leaves in two hours. If Walt and Eddy aren't answering the phone we need to figure out where they are."

"All right, let's give it a shot. But after the way she talked to me today I doubt that she will be very welcoming."

Jo cracked her knuckles. "Don't worry. I don't plan on being welcoming either."

Samantha hailed a cab and the two women hopped in. As the driver headed for Leila's address, Samantha couldn't ignore the uneasy feeling in the pit of her stomach. She tried Eddy's number again. Yet again there was no answer.

"Can you go any faster?" Samantha leaned forward.

"All right, but you're paying my speeding tickets." The driver stepped on the gas. As the cab tore down the road Samantha clenched her hands into fists.

"If that big meathead did anything to hurt either of them, I will make him pay."

Jo raised an eyebrow. "Feeling quite protective are we?"

"Someone has to protect them. They're always getting themselves into trouble."

"Good point." Jo nodded.

The cab pulled to a stop outside of Leila's house and Samantha paid the driver. "Can you wait, please?" Samantha stepped out of the cab. As soon as the two women were a few steps away from the cab the driver pulled off. "Wow, some driver." Samantha shook her head.

"Never mind that, look who is standing in the front yard."

"Leila." Samantha looked towards the woman. "I wonder how she is going to react."

"You!" Leila began to run towards both of them.

"Let me handle this, Samantha." Jo stepped in front of her.

Leila slowed and then stopped in front of Jo. "Where is he?"

"Where is who?" Jo fixed her with a glare.

"Where's Cory? I know that it has something to do with all of you."

"Yes, you might be right." Samantha stepped out from behind Jo. "And we want to know where our friends Walt and Eddy are. I'm guessing they're with Cory."

"But where are they?" Leila's hard stare softened with tears. "I haven't seen Cory all afternoon. I just know he went off somewhere with your friends. Where would he go? Did they arrest him? Are they going to hurt him?"

"No, to both." Samantha shook her head. "Eddy and Walt would not do anything to hurt Cory, and neither have the authority to arrest anyone. From what I understand they came here to ask about Mick. Do you know where Mick is?"

"Mick?" Leila's eyes drifted between the two women. "What do you mean? Why would they be asking about Mick?"

"Because Mick was on the train, too, Leila. He wasn't at work yesterday, because he was on the train." Samantha locked eyes with her to gauge her reaction. Leila's expression was blank until she began to put two and two together.

"He went on the train to protect Cory?"

"Or to back Cory up," Jo suggested. "Either way, it's very likely that's where Cory, Eddy, and Walt are. So, do you want to tell us where he might be?"

"He's probably at home." Leila rubbed at the curve of her cheek. "That must be where Cory is."

"Can you take us there?" Jo tried to gain the woman's attention. "It's very important, Leila. Our friends are missing, and your fiancé was the last person known to be with them."

"Why should I take you to them?" Leila glared at them. "You're trying to prove that one or both of them are murderers. So, why should I help you?"

"Because, Leila, if you don't take us to them and fast they might do something that they can't come back from. How far would Cory go to protect his father?" Samantha held the woman's gaze despite her dark stare.

"You're right." Leila shook her head. "He would do anything to protect his father. We need to get to them fast. Let's go." She walked towards her car. Jo grabbed Samantha's hand before she could follow after.

"What if she's working with them, Samantha? What if we walk right into a trap?"

"Do we have another choice? They have Walt and Eddy, we have no idea where or what they might have done with them. If we don't go with Leila we might never find them. Is that a risk we can take?"

"No. You're right." Jo sighed and released her hand. Once in the car the two braced themselves for whatever might come next.

Chapter Seventeen

When Leila pulled the car into the driveway of Mick's home, Samantha caught something out of the corner of her eye. It was another car that had pulled in a few driveways away. It was a populated street and so it shouldn't have struck her as unusual, but it did. Something about it held her attention until Leila opened the door.

"Mick's office is right down the corridor. I'm sure he can straighten all of this out," she said as she opened the office door.

"Cory no! Put that gun down!" Leila gasped as she rushed through the door. Jo and Samantha followed right on her heels.

"Close the door!" Cory snapped. "Or I take out this one." He pointed the gun at Walt.

"No!" Samantha growled. "Put that gun away!"

"Cory, this is crazy, you have to stop this." Mick started to stand up from his chair.

"Sit down, Dad! No way are you going to prison. For what? For that piece of garbage? No! You did the world a favor!"

Mick sank back down in his chair.

"Cory, calm down." Leila reached out to touch his arm. Cory jerked his arm back from her touch.

"I said, close the door, Leila!"

Leila jumped back and closed the door. Samantha and Jo stood close to each other as Eddy studied them both.

"This is getting out of hand, Cory, you need to let these women out of here." Eddy turned to look at the man with the gun.

"No. No one goes anywhere. I need to fix this." Cory gripped the gun tight in his hand.

"How is this going to fix anything?" Mick shook his head. "Cory, it's my fault, I did this."

"Did what?" Leila looked across the desk at him. "What is happening here? Please will someone tell me?"

Mick cleared his throat, then met Leila's eyes.

"I'm the one who killed Ryan, Leila. I'm sorry. It was an accident, but I'm the one who did it."

"What?" Leila's eyes widened. "Why! Why would you do that?"

"I didn't mean to I just didn't want him to hurt you, or Cory. I wanted you both to have the chance to have the happiness that you deserve. Is that really so wrong? Besides, it's not like I planned it. It just happened." He stared at his own hands with disbelief. "All I know for sure is that there is no way to go back. And this isn't the way to go forward. Cory, I need to pay for what I did."

"We're at an impasse, Cory. There's nowhere that you can go from here. Are you really going to kill us all?" Eddy stood up from his chair and looked straight at the man. "I don't think that you will. I think you know that you're in a tight spot, and the only way out is to put down that gun."

"Sit down." Cory released the safety on the gun. "I'm not asking anyone's opinion on this. You sit down while I figure it out."

Leila began to cry. "I'm sorry, Cory. This is all

my fault, I never should have brought you and your father into this drama with Ryan. I thought he was finally out of my life for good, now he's ruined everything."

"It doesn't have to be ruined." Samantha placed a hand on Leila's shoulder. "There's still a chance that this can be settled. Like Mick said, it was an accident, a good lawyer can help him prove that. As for Cory, he hasn't done anything that we can't all forget about. There is still an opportunity here to turn things around. Cory, don't you want to give Leila that chance? Are you going to take away the one person she truly loves?" Samantha turned her attention on Cory. Thick streams of sweat ran down his cheeks. He gripped the gun so tight that his hand shook. It was clear that he had never fired one before. "Cory, this isn't the way. Just put the gun down and we can figure this out together."

"No," Cory whispered the word. "I can't. My Dad was brave enough to protect me, now I have to be brave enough to protect him. Can't you see that?"

"Cory, all I can see is that you are hurting and you need help." Samantha moved towards him with cautious steps. "Leila's crying, your father is begging you to stop, no one here thinks that you're making a good choice right now. We know how much you love your father and Leila, you don't have to prove that to us."

"But it doesn't matter!" Cory held tightly to the gun. "It's all messed up now! Everything I was about to have, is gone! What is the point? So, what if four people die, I don't care. I need to make sure that my father stays out of jail." He aimed the gun directly at Samantha.

"No you don't!" Eddy jumped up and slid in front of Samantha. "I'm warning you now, boy, pointing a gun at this woman will guarantee my wrath. Lower you weapon, now."

Samantha's heart pounded as she prepared herself for the sound of a bullet being fired. When she didn't hear one, she peeked over Eddy's shoulder. Cory had lowered his weapon some, but not all the way.

"Cory no, please. Even if you were to kill them all, I promise you, I would still turn myself into the police. I couldn't live with the burden of one life on my conscience, please don't add four more."

Before Cory could answer his father, the glass of the office window broke. A canister was tossed inside and began to spread smoke as soon as it hit the floor. Eddy took the opportunity to lunge at Cory. Cory was so disoriented by the smoke that he didn't realize what Eddy was doing until it was too late. Eddy wrestled the gun from his hand and backed off fast.

"Everybody out!" Eddy pointed towards the door. "I don't know what's in that smoke."

"Who's out there?" Samantha lifted her shirt collar to cover her nose and mouth. "What are we walking out into?"

"I don't know, but it has to be better than here." Jo placed a hand on Samantha's shoulder and the two made their way out of the room. Leila followed behind them.

"Cory, Mick, let's go!" She called back into the smoke. Mick emerged from the room but Cory was nowhere to be seen.

Walt was the last one through the door. He coughed and waved his hand in front of his face. "Horrible smell, really."

"Are you all right?" Samantha nearly passed out on the spot as the voice spoke up a few inches from her ear. She jumped back and turned to see Peter.

"Peter! What are you doing here?"

"I was looking out for my client. I wanted to find out who actually killed Ryan. So, I've had my eye on these two. I saw everyone go in and then not come out. When I looked in the window I saw that you were being held hostage."

"And you just happened to have a smoke bomb?" Eddy looked at him with a raised eyebrow.

"It's a tool of the trade. I have some great

supplier connections from being on the force. With the crimes I investigate I have a lot of tools at my disposal."

"Wait, where's Cory?" Leila turned back towards the room. The smoke had cleared, but there was no sign of Cory.

"He must have taken off." Eddy shook his head. "I guess he can't face what's happened here."

Leila hugged Mick and looked into his eyes. "I know why you did it, and even though I don't condone it, I know that you did it for Cory and me."

"I'm sorry, Leila. I wish I had never gotten on that train."

"But you did." Peter held out a set of handcuffs. "I can take you in myself if you want. I can help you explain what happened."

"You would do that?" Mick's eyes widened with gratitude.

"Yours isn't the only life that Ryan ruined,

Mick. But, you made a terrible mistake and you'll have to face the consequences."

"I know." Mick lowered his eyes. He folded his hands behind his back. Peter handcuffed him and led him to his car.

Once Mick was settled in the backseat Peter turned to face Samantha, Jo, Eddy, and Walt. "In case you were wondering, I'm not a murderer." He winked at Samantha and then got into the car. Samantha felt her heart sink.

"Don't worry, you weren't wrong to suspect him." Eddy placed a hand on her shoulder. "All of the elements were there. Money, family, and experience in life and death situations. He was the perfect suspect."

"Maybe," Samantha sighed. "But he was also once my friend, and maybe if I had taken more time to listen to him, to give him a reason to trust me, I would still be able to count him as a friend."

Eddy chuckled and squeezed her shoulder. "That's where you're wrong, Samantha."

"What do you mean?"

Eddy tilted his head towards Peter's car as it pulled away. "That man never had any interest in being your friend. He was, and probably still is in love with you, Samantha. Nothing you do can change that."

Samantha rolled her eyes. "You're way off on that one, Eddy."

"If you say so." He shrugged.

"People! We're going to be late!" Walt urged them towards the street. "We have to go right this second."

"I guess we better call another cab," Eddy said.

"Anything other than a police car." Walt sighed.

"When were you in a police car?" Jo raised an eyebrow.

"Don't worry, we'll have plenty of time to talk about it on the way home." Eddy pulled out his phone to call a cab.

"Love is a really funny thing isn't it." Samantha looked over at Jo. "Love of family, love of a romantic partner, it makes people crazy."

"Maybe." Jo frowned. "But from what I hear, it's worth it."

"Don't believe it, it's all chemicals and endorphins." Walt began to lecture them both.

"Oh yes, it's going to be a very long trip back to Sage Gardens." Samantha laughed.

The End

More Cozy Mysteries by Cindy Bell

Sage Gardens Cozy Mysteries

Birthdays Can Be Deadly

Money Can Be Deadly

Trust Can Be Deadly

Ties Can Be Deadly

Chocolate Centered Cozy Mysteries

The Sweet Smell of Murder

Dune House Cozy Mysteries

Seaside Secrets

Boats and Bad Guys

Treasured History

Hidden Hideaways

Dodgy Dealings

Suspects and Surprises

Heavenly Highland Inn Cozy Mysteries

Murdering the Roses

Dead in the Daisies

Killing the Carnations

Drowning the Daffodils

Suffocating the Sunflowers

Books, Bullets and Blooms

A Deadly serious Gardening Contest

A Bridal Bouquet and a Body

Wendy the Wedding Planner Cozy Mysteries

Matrimony, Money and Murder

Chefs, Ceremonies and Crimes

Knives and Nuptials

Mice, Marriage and Murder

Made in the USA
Coppell, TX
07 August 2020